THE LAST MAGNOLIA

A.G. MORENO

outskirts press

Outskirts Press, Inc.
http://www.outskirtspress.com

Paperback ISBN: 978-1-9772-4170-2
Hardback ISBN: 978-1-9772-4288-4

Cover Image by Epifanio Moreno

PRINTED IN THE UNITED STATES OF AMERICA

To my wonderful hubster Epifanio, I am so grateful for all you do for our family. I am honored to be your wife and best friend. You mean the world to me, my love. Thank you for designing and creating the cover. It is so beautiful. You are an amazing artist and I'll always be your #1 fan. To my kiddos, I adore you two. Thank you for being the most loving, the kindest and the most pure-hearted children a mom could ever ask for. The "chocolate cake secret" will always bring a smile to my face and laughter to my heart (LMBO). To my Dad, not a day goes by that I don't think ever so fondly of the very special bond we shared. Oh, how I wish you were still here to take me to the zoo. I love and miss you so much. Rest in peace Daddy. You will be in my heart always.

1

THE FACADE

She was convinced the sun hated her. It was clearly playing some type of cruel joke all while providing her with a scathing, falsified sense of optimism and security. Today, Annabella's ultraviolet companion seemed to be smiling at her similar to the manner in which it did when endearingly depicted by an innocent, young child upon an artistic endeavor. Rather than merely flying, the birds were gliding through the air only to land atop the greenest and tallest of trees. They were also a part this charade- singing and chirping so purely and melodically. Upon her awakening, Annabella immediately foresaw a clear path of contentment and elation. This was indeed uncommon of most of her days' beginnings, especially considering the fact she was probably as opposite a morning person that anyone could imagine a seven-year-old to be. She wasn't groggy nor dreading a mundane rest of the day which was shocking bearing in mind the amount of rest she had gotten the night prior was limited at best. After brushing her teeth and washing the sleepiness from her eyes, Annabella went to her closet to choose an outfit for the day. Nearly every item in her wardrobe was pink. What struck some as odd about her love for the stereotypically, overly feminine color was that Annabella wasn't the delicate type. She hated wearing dresses, especially the frilly kind. She was quite content with adorning herself in a pair of magenta pants, a pink shirt and some matching footwear. The dresses her mother would insist upon never suited her at all. There was always a little skirt or dress with a 'can-can' underneath that would itch to high Heaven. Her mother always wanted Annabella to look like a little lady or some horrid, warped notion of regality. Annabella never understood what was lady-like about publicly scratching one's own butt in any setting, public or private. It was just unnatural and uncomfortable. Annabella honestly held the conviction that her mother had a mission to get rid of her tomboy exterior one way or another.

Annabella had a great day at school. She aced her Spelling test, they served an actually edible meal in the cafeteria and she and her best friend were the first ones at the swings instead of that annoyingly cute girl with the pigtails who never ate lunch so she could beat everyone else outside to take part in the only acceptable activity instilled upon such a lackluster playground. Annabella's mother, Ronda picked her up from school as she almost always did. She would often do so in a different car nearly every week due to her boss, Mr. Abel at the car dealership, allowing her to drive some of the cars off the lot and oftentimes, even keep them overnight or longer. Annabella always thought Mr. Abel had sort of a thing for her mother. He was married but from what Annabella had seen within her young life, that didn't seem to stop most men anyhow. Mr. Abel had been burned very badly in a house fire and rumor had it that his wife had been having an affair due to him no longer having the handsome, dapper appearance that many women once fawned over. Mr. Abel seemed to look at Ronda with a grin that implied that if she had been so inclined, he would have gladly taken things far beyond a typically professional level. Many men would not have blamed him for having such emotions. Ronda was a very pretty woman with smooth chestnut skin, dark hair, dimples and a tiny birth mark above her lip, sort of like Marilyn Monroe. She was also quite petite- just under five feet tall. She seemed to suffer from some insecurities regarding her stature, hence her fiery demeanor and her constant, undeniable obsession with high-heeled shoes. In Annabella's opinion, Ronda being so little actually worked well in her favor. After all, men do like to feel big, strong and dominant and what could make a man feel more masculine than to cradle a small woman in his arms?

Annabella got into the car with an immense grin on her face. The sky seemed bluer and clearer than ever. Her mother, on the other hand, didn't seem to share her enthusiasm. Then again, she was not what one would consider a generally happy, jovial person. She did not smile very often and sometimes, she often seemed to prefer to be unhappy. They would take family vacations; Ronda would find a reason to start a fight with Annabella's dad. They'd go to dinner; she'd find motivation to make the outing uncomfortable. Why would someone who had happiness, stability and love all around them rather bask in their own gloom? Once they had been driving for some time, Annabella turned on the radio. One of her favorite songs was playing. She began to sing along but was met by a protesting eye roll. The point was well received hence the decision to hum and bob her head instead. For some reason, this seemed to annoy Ronda just as much and maybe even more causing her to look menacingly at Annabella and turn the knob of the radio with so much quickness and force, it could have easily loosened and broken from the console. Annabella took this as her cue to simply refrain from making any more sounds that may have been disturbing or irritating to her mother's apparently sensitive ears. When Ronda was angry, most that knew her understood that it was best to simply be quiet and let it pass. So what if she didn't have her song? She had her beautiful sun to clothe her face in its stunning warmth. Annabella put her head out the window and enjoyed the rest of the ride home in silence. This wasn't at all surprising to Annabella. She and her mother never had too much to talk about. One thing that Annabella and her mother *did* love to do together was eat 'Laffy Taffy' candy. Ronda loved listening to Annabella read the jokes. The puns absolutely tickled them both. Their mutual enjoyment of one another hardly occurred and never lasted long though. Annabella always wanted to have a stronger mother-daughter bond but there wasn't much she could do to change the way Ronda felt about her. Annabella believed she was loved or at least tolerated in the archetypal, obligated sense but there was certainly something missing- something that Annabella couldn't quite figure out.

As they turned on their street, Annabella noticed that a few of their neighbors hadn't cut their lawns in quite some time. Annabella was always very observant of lawns. This was largely because her dad was very picky when it came to their own grass. He always made sure that there were no rocks and/or leaves on the lawn and that it was always crisp and fresh. Annabella agreed and also believed that a nice front lawn made all the difference in the overall appearance of a home. Annabella chuckled at the thought of her brother disagreeing and griping when it was time to help their father with the landscaping. They pulled into the driveway. Ronda still hadn't said a word to her, but

Annabella didn't harp on it. She didn't have any homework that day so Annabella thought she'd go in the backyard and play on her swing set for a little while. She didn't want to end such a beautiful, sunny day by going inside too early. Annabella absolutely adored her swing set. It was pink and blue; it had two swings, a slide, one teeter totter, monkey bars and one big porch swing. Her dad had gotten it for her along with a weight bench for her brother who claimed he wanted to bulk up his incredibly scrawny twelve and a half-year-old physique. Her dad worked all night putting it together. Annabella spent most of the time she was home playing on and enjoying it. She could never quite get completely across the monkey bars though. From her father, she had inherited incredibly sweaty hands that wouldn't allow her to firmly grip the bars. Plus, she hadn't adopted the upper body strength that was clearly needed to achieve such a feat. Mid-play, she got thirsty and went inside to get some juice from the refrigerator. Dinah and Joshua were sitting at the kitchen table. Annabella always found it funny that she was the only one of the three without a biblical name but she loved her title nonetheless. Annabella had such a pretty ring to it and besides, she appreciated the sense of uniqueness it supplied her with. Dinah was close to nine years older than Annabella. She and her sister were extremely close despite the substantial age gap. Over the years, Dinah had helped get Annabella dressed for school and often allowed her to sleep in her bed when she and Joshua would let her watch scary movies with them. None of them were actually allowed to view such films inside their home or otherwise. Their family belonged to a religion where watching horror movies was correlated with being obsessed or fascinated with the Devil and his impish counterparts. While their faith's disapproval and disdain only added to Annabella's curiosity, it also supplemented her fear, causing her to feel that after she watched such a movie, said "fascination" would cause these wicked creatures to come and pay her a visit as "thanks" for being so interested in what they had to offer. What she and her siblings found strange is that their parents, especially their mother along with the rest of the members of this religious organization, were the main ones constantly discussing the Devil and the end of the world. Certainly, Annabella watching a movie with the Boogeyman hiding within an adolescent's closet didn't draw a parallel to her wanting to greet Lucifer himself and partake in some sort of midnight rendezvous. Joshua teased her constantly about being such a "scaredy-cat". In fact, he typically taunted her for nothing at all. Today was no different. "Hey Smelly Annabelly!" he shouted. He could be so immature sometimes. "Shut up Josh!" Annabella replied. Joshua asked her if she'd heard the news. "What news?" she asked. "Mama and Daddy are getting a divorce." Annabella knew what a divorce was and had watched enough movies and television to know that it meant that her mother and father did not want to be together any longer. Annabella should've known her time on cloud nine wouldn't last long. What she *did* comprehend though, was that this one sentence out of Joshua's mouth would change her and her family's entire existence as they knew it.

2

SCORCHING SERENITY

Annabella never thought she'd be talking with her father, her own flesh and blood through bars. She just wanted him to give her one of those big, nearly suffocating bear hugs that only he could so efficiently supply. Annabella loved her father. He was 6'6", muscular and looked like he belonged on the set of a soap opera. He was very charming and strong but he was also bust-a-gut funny and despite his large stature, he was actually a very kind and loving person. He had fought in Vietnam twice and was a very proud Veteran. Annabella's mother had also served in the Army. This is where they met. Ronda was not Annabella's dad's first wife. He had been married before and had two daughters and a son with his first wife. Tragically, one of their daughters had passed away as a baby due to premature birth complications. Annabella's mother was part of if not the main reason for the demise of his initial union. While William was indeed responsible for keeping his own nether regions under wraps as a married man, Annabella had watched many romance movies and she somewhat understood that temptation was a real thing and a moment of passion could come in an instant and completely throw morals and the feelings of others entirely out of the window. Annabella's father thought Ronda was the cutest thing he had ever seen. She had spunk and that's what he liked most about her. Annabella also thought that he liked her mother's country background. She was from a small town in Arkansas called Grandburg- a city with less than 3,500 people. Annabella recalled taking trips there and her father often staying behind because the house that Ronda grew up in was so small, it made him feel like he was living a real-life "Gulliver's Travels". Ronda had a big family. Her father was a retired military cook, her mother, a housewife. She had seven siblings total- six sisters and one brother. Annabella's grandfather had started a small farm on the property. He had chickens, a few goats and a cow that he later had to slaughter. He grew his own fruits and vegetables as well. He had quite the green thumb. What Annabella loved most about her 'Paw-paw' was the way he talked. He was missing a great deal of teeth, largely due to his love of non-filtered cigarettes and soda or "pop" as they called it. She could never fully grasp what he said most of the time on account of his raspy voice and thick, southern drawl but she just loved listening to him go on and on about absolutely nothing at all. She had never seen live chickens in real life back in the city. The only time Annabella saw a chicken in New Orleans was when it was in a box of "Popeye's" or covered in some type of rich and spicy sauce. The very first thing she would do when she got there was ask him, "Paw-paw, can I go see the chickens... Pleeeeeeaaase?" After the first two visits or so, she no longer had to ask and it just became "their thing". Annabella's grandmother was a very lovely woman. She looked like a Native American chief, only female and much prettier. She'd always wear her long hair in two big braids split down the middle. They say she was mixed with Native

American blood, but then again it was quite commonplace for many Black people to say that although there was no true knowledge or proof of such ancestry. Annabella believed her grandmother was half-White but then again, she had never met her great-grandmother and relying on her own family for factual details was like relying on 'Paw-paw' to win a corn on the cob eating contest. Annabella and her grandmother never had too many verbal exchanges. 'Maw-maw' just never seemed that interested in getting to know her. Annabella just took it for what it was and she loved her just the same. Annabella loved seeing her Aunts-especially her Aunt Shirley and her daughter, Nadine. Nadine was pretty, smart and always seemed to want to help everyone. Annabella knew *she'd* make it out of Grandburg and do something productive with her life. Annabella missed the days of visiting her mother's family but as time went on, those days became few and far between.

The family never really spent time with Annabella's father's side of the family which never made much sense considering they lived only about an hour away in Mississippi. Josiah Garland was William's father. He was a welder by trade but he could fix, restore and build almost anything. According to Annabella's dad, Josiah was one of the meanest men one could ever come across. Some may have believed that being a tough, strict father was reasonably necessary with four boys and two girls in the '50s and '60s, but from William's and a few others' descriptions, 'Big Jo' would often go far beyond the point of typical discipline. William was always the feistiest of all the sons. This may have been because it was simply in his nature, or it could have been that 'Big Jo' was always provoking antagonistic disputes. He would set up fights in the yard being sure to make certain William was always outnumbered. William often thought that he was being singled out simply because he was one of the lighter skinned of the children. 'Big Jo' often made comments about William belonging to "the Milkman". This was of course absurd considering Grandma Gloria was Louisiana Creole and all her children had similar features. Additionally, Gloria worshipped the ground 'Big Jo' walked on and was terrified to merely even speak a word against him let alone go outside of their marriage. There seemed to be some jealousy issues hidden beneath the surface. Everyone feared 'Big Jo' except for William and if he did, he never showed it. This only infuriated 'Big Jo' and brought about numerous attempts to break William and weaken him just as he did most individuals he crossed paths with. In William's opinion, the only things 'Big Jo' ever did for him was supply him with the necessities and aggressively pass on his capabilities of being incredibly intricate and effective with his hands. There were never any forms of affection exchanged between them and although there had been many negative occurrences among the father and son, one incident would cause William and 'Big Jo's' relationship to go from estranged to destroyed beyond repair.

William came straight home after school every day. He was far from a goody two-shoes but Gloria worried about her children while they were away from the house-especially during times of blatant racism and violence against people of color in those days. William wasn't afraid of anything but the last thing he wanted to do was bring upon extra stress to his mother's already fragile heart. William had been the only student in his 7th grade class to make an 'A' on his Math test. He was wise beyond his years. He had a certain charm and wit about him even then. This also angered Big Jo since back in *his* day; it was unheard of for young men to do anything other than work and support their wives and children at a young age rather than remain single and focus on an academic future. William came home in a great mood. He kissed his mother on the cheek as she stirred a giant pot of chili. Big Jo was smoking his cigar in the living room while rocking back & forth in the only chair that was strictly off limits to the rest of the house's members. "Taste this baby!" Grandma Gloria said to William. "It could use a little more spice Mama." "I thought so too but your father said it was just right." "I'll add a few more peppers." Gloria had no idea that 'Big Jo' had heard their entire exchange but William knew that it had angered his father. He just didn't know how much.

William offered to help his mother clear the table and do the dishes. He saw how hard his mother worked to keep up their home and he felt badly that no one would ever offer to help her do anything around the house. The children that were old enough to assist her were often too lazy or too afraid to do anything that might annoy 'Big Jo' since he felt that it was Gloria's sole duty to complete each and every household chore without any help from anyone, especially him. "That chili sure was good Ma!" "Nice and spicy just like I like it!" uttered William as he wiped his mouth. "I'm making gumbo next week" his mother said. "Mmmmm my favorite! Can't wait!" As William turned away from his mother, he saw a puff of smoke in the darkened doorway. Not thinking too much of it, he told his mother to go on to bed and he would finish cleaning up. William wiped down the counter then headed outside to take the trash to the big garbage can. He loved the humidity in the air. The atmosphere always felt like it was just about to rain and the smell of the dew on the grass was almost hypnotizing. William took a deep, cleansing breath and headed back inside. He was getting tired and wanted to get to bed so he could have a good start to his morning. He had always been an early bird. William walked back inside. He only reached his arm in to turn off the lights since he hadn't planned on going back into the kitchen. "Come here boy!", 'Big Jo' screamed. William's heart sank.

Reluctantly, William walked all the way into the kitchen. "Sit yo red ass down!" In southern states, especially Mississippi and Louisiana, referring to someone as being "red" meant that the person had a lighter hue to their skin. William sat down. Next to 'Big Jo' was a crate of leftover chili peppers that Gloria hadn't used. Big Jo twiddled one between his fingers. "I guess you think you funny huh?" "What di....?" "Shut up!" Big Jo shouted. "You know damn well I don't like my food too God damn spicy!" "But *you* do don'tcha?" "Well show me how spicy you like it boy!" Big Jo placed two peppers in the center of the table. "Why does he hate me so much?" William thought. He considered not eating them but he knew if he didn't, things would only get worse for him, his siblings and likely even his mother. After all, he thought he could handle two peppers. He grabbed the first one and stared at his father as he lit his cigar with a menacing grin. "He's enjoying this" thought William. Determined not to give 'Big Jo' the satisfaction of seeing him in pain, William ate both peppers without as little as a grimace. At the time, he was so Hell bent on not letting his father win, he had just managed to seal a horrible fate for himself. "Oh, so you a man now?" "I'mma show you who the man is around here!" Big Jo struck William with a blow so hard it knocked him from his seat. "Getcho ass back in that chair!" All the ruckus must have disturbed Gloria because she shuffled into the kitchen wearing her robe and slippers. "What's going on Jo?" "Stay out of this Gloria! I mean it!" She was so afraid of her husband she didn't know how to put an end to what was happening. "You wanna be tough? Eat em ALL then!" Big Jo began shoving the peppers into William's bloody, already flaming hot mouth. There must have been eight or nine total. "You don't chew em up, I'mma give you the worst damn beatin' you ever had in your damn life boy!" William wasn't too worried about himself but as Gloria stepped forward to try and help her son, 'Big Jo' grabbed her by her hair. "This is your fault, you little bitch!" William closed his eyes, chewed the peppers and swallowed them within seconds. His mouth was now seemingly on fire. He ran to the sink to get water and was met with a slam to the ground and a foot on the back of his neck. That's all William could remember before blacking out. He dreamed of a better tomorrow, of being an adult who no longer had to be subjected to so much pain, such hatred. All William wanted was love. He would've even settled for normalcy. Sadly, fantasies and dreams were all he had at that moment.

William was awoken abruptly. "Baby, wake up!" "You gotta get out of here!" William felt so sick he got up and ran past his mother. He sat upon the commode with his head in his hands. He felt hot and cold all at the same time. He was so afraid to use the restroom because he knew it would be painful. He managed to finish with tears in his eyes and an inferno in his belly. He couldn't bear to take toilet paper to his backside due to the pain. He just wanted a cold shower. As he rose and went to flush, he saw something he'd never seen before. The toilet was filled with blood. William began shouting, "Mama, mama!" Gloria ran to the bathroom and saw her son curled up into a knot on the bathroom floor. She knew she needed to do something and she needed to do it fast. 'Big Jo' had left for work but Gloria knew that he could pop up at any moment to check up on things. Luckily, the children who still lived at home had been at a relative's house and did not have to witness or endure any part of the prior night's horror. Gloria had already packed a bag for William. "Let's get you cleaned up." She helped him into the shower and stepped outside to keep an eye out for 'Big Jo'. William came out of that shower a different person. The last glimmer in his eyes was now gone. He seemed to feel nothing at all. "I love you baby and I'm so sorry but he'll never hurt you again, I promise." "You're gonna stay with my sister Mable and her husband in New Orleans until we can figure things out." "Figure things out?" William thought. "What was there to figure out?" 'Big Jo' surely had the Devil inside him and he was only becoming more ominous. William knew 'Big Jo' would kill him but yet he worried for his mother and younger siblings. "He only goes this far with you and I don't know why" said Gloria. She kissed William's cheeks and hugged him tighter than she ever had before. A yellow taxicab was parked down the street as not to draw attention to the house in case 'Big Jo' showed up. William kissed his mother and ran all the way to the cab, without a glance behind him.

Surprisingly, Big Jo's frequent abuse and the tormenting of his family was not the only aspect that made the lives of William, his siblings, and mother more difficult to bear. After William had moved away, one of his brothers would write him and inform him of what was going on back in Mississippi. During a small family gathering, there was an implication that one of their female cousins was in fact, not their cousin, but instead, rumor had it that she was actually their sister. While 'Big Jo' did seem to take more kindly to the girls in the family, he was never what anyone would've deemed a nice or caring person. However, there were two members of the family that he seemed to treat very caringly no matter what type of mood he was in. 'Big Jo' would fawn over how beautiful and smart Valerie was nearly to the jealousy and sometimes disgust of everyone around. He also had a very close relationship with her mother Shantell who was the wife of his second to oldest son, George. They would giggle at their own secret jokes, he'd compliment her figure or her hair and she'd always find some sort of way to be alone with him whether it was going to the store or going outside with him while he puffed on a cigar. During Shantell's pregnancy, he would give up his seat so that she could rest her feet. He would even talk to her belly—something he never did with Gloria during any of her pregnancies. Valerie looked a lot like 'Big Jo' and even had many of his mannerisms and as much as everyone thought it, no one dared to ever bring it to 'Big Jo's attention for fear that they'd then become a target. No one wanted to give 'Big Jo' a reason to put them on his bad side so they bottled it in and with time, put it away in their minds, never to even whisper it again. Other stories of inappropriate behavior among one of William's younger brothers and a female cousin also surfaced but perhaps hoping and not wanting it to be true eventually made those tales disappear as well. For William, however, the nightmares never seemed to go away. He was simply happy that he was allowed to begin a new life and get away from it all.

William's Aunt Mable and her husband Alfred were very kind. They didn't have any children so they gladly treated William as their own. They knew that he had already been through so much and they wanted to make his stay with them as loving as possible. While Gloria was a lovely woman and tried to be the best mother she could be to her children, her fear and the interference of 'Big Jo' made it nearly impossible to bring them up with the warmth and love that she had set out to all along. Mable and Alfred showed William what a marriage should look like. They worked together as partners and treated William as a member of the family instead of merely a fixture within it. Sadly though, William was deeply scarred from what had happened to him and he never truly healed from the torment he underwent at the hands of his father.

3

UNINVITED

Annabella failed to understand how anyone could ever be so vile toward their own family. Yet, at that moment, she could see inklings of what would later become commonplace in her own household. Annabella saw her dad's truck pull into the driveway. Immediately, a smile shone across her face. She knew *he* could give her some answers. Her father always knew just what to say. She ran to the door but was stopped by the locked burglar bars that her mother and father had insisted on installing on every home since the break-in that occurred when Annabella was four years old. "Hey Belly! Open the door baby!" William said excitedly. "Okay Daddy! I just need to get the key." William had nicknamed her 'Belly' when she was just a baby. One night, he was holding Annabella and she was crying uncontrollably. He tried everything to get her to stop. Nothing he did seemed to help so in a last-ditch effort, he resorted to making silly faces. When his attempts failed, William, who was completely exhausted, nearly wanted to cry himself. William believed that Annabella could sense this because she immediately stopped crying and suddenly made a super funny face back at him. William claimed that it was the biggest, longest 'belly laugh' he ever had. Hence, the nickname, 'Belly' was born. Many close friends and family members called Annabella by that name but oddly, Ronda never quite took to the moniker.

Annabella ran upstairs to tell Ronda that William was there. Ronda arose leisurely and gave Annabella a bit of an eye roll. "Mom, are you okay?" "I'm fine Annabella" she replied smugly. After what seemed like an eternity, she finally came downstairs to the door. "What do you want William?" "Well, I'd like to see my children and get the rest of my things if that's okay with you. "I gave you everything you're gonna get outta here." "You know what Ronda? I'm not even gonna do this with you. Can you just open the door so I can see the kids?" Ronda walked toward the kitchen where Dinah and Joshua were still sitting. They had these smirks on their faces that Annabella couldn't quite figure out. They didn't seem to want to see their father. Perhaps Ronda could feel this and rather than look for the keys, she walked right back to the door and said that she still didn't know where she'd left them. Annabella continued to look through the bars like a lost puppy. "Are you gonna sleep home tonight?" "Not tonight baby girl." "Well, can I go around the house through the gate so I can give you a hug?" Annabella asked. "The gate's locked and I ain't about to look all around for them damn keys either." Ronda exclaimed. "But wh...?" Annabella attempted to ask. "I'll come pick you up this weekend. Okay kiddo?" "But I don't understand..." Annabella only wanted to give her father a hug and maybe ask him to stay for dinner. Was that too much to ask? Things were beginning to change already. Annabella knew divorce would mean change but she always thought she'd be able to see her father and hug him whenever she wanted to. Maybe divorce was more serious than she had once believed.

Weeks passed and things around the house only became more grim. Dinah spent most of her time on the phone talking to her boyfriend, Craig which is something she'd previously always had to sneak around to do. Now, she didn't try to hide it. She even seemed to attempt to flaunt her newfound freedom in a way. Ronda only got out of the bed to meet necessities and Joshua didn't seem to pay Annabella much attention at all, not even to tease her. The next day, after picking her up from school, Ronda told Annabella that they would be moving and she would need to start packing up her stuff. "Moving where?" Annabella thought. She loved their house. Her room was perfect. The paint was pink & white, there were pictures of puppies and kittens on the walls and her enormous closet was full of awesome clothes and toys. And what about her swing set? Surely they wouldn't be able to take it with them. Annabella held 'Fancy' close to her. 'Fancy' was the puppy her father had gotten her. She still remembered the moment like it was yesterday. Annabella had begged her dad for a puppy for months. He always seemed to be disinterested or preoccupied when she would bring it up and honestly, Annabella thought it was never going to happen. Until one night as she was getting ready for bed, she heard her father's truck pull into the driveway. Annabella was waiting until he came inside so she could say goodnight. He called Ronda outside and after fiddling around in William's truck for a bit, Ronda came back in and told Annabella to go right upstairs. A little confused as to why her father didn't want to see her at that moment, she hesitantly headed up the steps. As she pulled the covers over her head and attempted to go to sleep, she heard footsteps coming up the stairs. She saw her father standing in the doorway. He flicked on the lights and in his arms was the most adorable, gray and white Pomeranian that anyone ever saw. She even had a pink bow in her hair and a pink pedicure on all her delightful little toes! Annabella immediately jumped from her bed and began to cry. She was perfect. Annabella actually got so excited; her nose began to bleed which had never happened before. After stopping the nose fountain and somewhat gaining her composure, Annabella asked her dad if 'Fancy' could sleep in her bed. Normally, the answer would have been an immediate "no" but the look on her face would've brought any man to his knees. "Alright, but just for tonight." "Ok Daddy, I love you so much! Thank you, thank you!" Annabella hugged him tighter than ever and fell asleep. It was one of the greatest days of her life. Unfortunately, she now wondered if it had been one of her last.

Annabella was not at all as exuberant as she had been days ago. She completed her schoolwork as if she were a zombie still in possession of half a brain. She felt as if a big piece of her life had been swapped with a less fortunate portion of someone else's. Her best friend Suzette tried making her laugh only to get a smirk and a distant look. "What's the matter?" Suzette questioned. "I don't want to talk about it right now Suzie." Annabella had always taken pride in her family. She loved talking about their many trips and vacations and she would always have a funny story to tell afterwards. One time, they had gone to the Riverwalk and once outside, as they often did, William and Joshua decided to have a foot race. This was entertaining in itself considering that William could have probably walked at a normal pace and still beaten Joshua. They lined up as they always had and picked their finish line which was a light post at the middle of the street. Dinah yelled, "On your mark, get set, go!" They both took off at full speed with William unsurprisingly in the lead. Suddenly, there was a "click clack" noise.

Annabella, Joshua and the rest of the family looked toward the sound only to see William, this tall statuesque man, standing there with his break-away pants nearly completely undone wearing, some cheetah-print, extremely form-fitting bikini underwear. Ronda ran over and tried to help, but it was too late. The roaring laughter that ensued could have awakened the dead. It continued all the way home and was a moment that they'd never forget nor ever let William live down.

Annabella knew those moments would probably be diminished or maybe even disappear altogether. This made her anxious and her stomach began to ache. She raised her hand and asked Mrs. Vanderski if she could be excused to use the restroom. Mrs. V did not like Annabella. She felt as though Annabella was a smart aleck with no respect for authority whatsoever. This was certainly not the case and all of Annabella's previous teachers would have easily and happily vouched for her. Annabella believed that one classroom incident must have been the final culprit in Mrs. V's disdain for her. The class had to read a story aloud about an African American family that took place shortly after slavery. Naturally, the type of language being spoken in the tale was not one that many would have considered "proper English" but this should have been expected and perhaps the book may have not been appropriate for students lacking the maturity level to understand this notion. One of the White, male students stood up when his turn to read came and said, "I can't read this kind of story because my parents don't like for me to talk Black talk." Annabella looked at Mrs. V and expected her to correct, educate him and explain that the story was important to American History and that there were reasons behind the way the people in the story talked but instead she simply said, "OK David, go ahead and close your book and study your Spelling words." Annabella didn't think this was the right choice as an educator nor did she think it was a fair thing to do. Therefore, when it was Annabella's turn to read aloud, she stood up and said, "My parents don't want me to talk Black talk either." This was actually true in a sense because Annabella's father always insisted that the children speak proper English. Still, Annabella understood and actually was enjoying the story very much before David's snide remark. Mrs. V did not give Annabella the same courtesy or treatment and insisted on sending Annabella to the Principal's office and calling her parents. Vanderski scheduled a parent-teacher conference for a couple of days later. "That girl is out of control!" Ronda yelled into the phone receiver. "No, she isn't Ronda but all this must be hard on the kids". William replied. "Dinah and Joshua are fine. Annabella is the only one acting out." "She always *has* been the difficult one" Ronda replied. "She's not difficult to *me*." William responded. "That's because you baby her." "Do you know that damn teacher had the nerve to ask me if there was something going on at home?" yelled Ronda. "Well, what did you tell her?" asked William. "Nothing! I don't want that White woman to know all my damn business!" "So, you'd rather her think that Belly is an unlikable, bad child instead?" "This is her last year at that school as far as I'm concerned. I'll enroll her somewhere else next year" Ronda concluded. "Fine Ronda, if that's what you want." Neither parent attended the parent-teacher conference.

To Annabella's surprise, instead of her mom's car waiting for her after the bell rang at the day's closing, she saw her Dad's blue truck. She loved that truck. In fact, everyone did. It was full of nearly all the amenities one could think of. It had a TV, a cellular phone, a radar detector and the outside was covered in lights that made it look like a spaceship cruising down a dark street. Annabella ran over and hopped in. "Hey Daddy!" "Hey baby girl! How was your day?" It was ok Daddy but I still don't know why you can't come in the house anymore." "There are some things about adults that you'll probably never understand until you become one yourself" he said. "I just want you to know something though. None of this will ever change the way I feel about you, your sister and your brother. Okay?" "I know." Annabella said somberly. "Let's not talk about it right now though because your mom doesn't want you to stay out too late because it's a school day." After they got something to eat and visited Annabella's uncle, William drove her home. On the way, Annabella asked him "Are you gonna come in?" "I think I need to give your mom a little bit more time before I try to do that again." William explained. "Well, what did you do to her?" "Why don't you want to be married to her anymore?" Annabella asked. "Belly, I love your mother very much but things just aren't the same anymore and just because you love someone, it doesn't mean that you have to be married to them" William responded. Annabella was young but she just wanted a direct answer, a real answer. Annabella knew that people didn't just get divorced for nothing but according to her mother, that's exactly what had happened. Ronda had told the children that she and William were simply lying in bed and William basically turned over and said, "I want a divorce." Annabella still believed that it could not have simply been a sudden occurrence and that there must have been signs that would've clearly pointed to the marriage's ultimate demise. Joshua and Dinah seemed to take their mother's account at face value. In fact, they seemed to be happy that this was all happening. They were at an age where they wanted to hang out with their friends more than their family. They wanted to date and experience the world and it seemed as though they wanted to do so at any cost. Annabella appeared to be the only one apprehensive and curious about why it was ending. Perhaps it was because she had always been an observant child or maybe it was because she wanted to mend her family. Either way, she wasn't just going to stand by and let everything fall apart without even an inkling of an idea why.

4

BEGINNING'S END

Moving day had come and Annabella was almost done packing up her things. Still uncertain where they were all going, she did so hesitantly. Ronda had become more standoffish and quite frankly, she was changing more with each passing day. Annabella felt for her. Even despite Ronda's rough demeanor, Annabella knew her mother must've been hurting inside. As Annabella folded some clothes and put them into boxes, she thought of 'Fancy'. Ronda had already given her away. Although Ronda relished in the act of showing off the designer dog to everyone, in Annabella's eyes she seemed a little too eager to rid herself of their family pet. It was likely because getting her in the first place was William's idea. Annabella began to cry. Suddenly, Joshua walked in. "You okay?" he asked. "No. I miss 'Fancy" and I don't wanna move! I love it here." "I know, but that's what happens in a divorce. It'll be alright." "You can come in my room and help me defeat the evil King. I'm almost at the last level." Usually, Annabella would've been ecstatic but today, she just wasn't in the mood. That night, they piled into the car and were onward to their new home.

As they drove, Annabella thought, "Maybe it won't be so bad. Both my parents have great taste and I'm sure this place will be lovely, even if Dad isn't there all the time." After about a 20-minute drive, they pulled into a parking lot that bore quite the resemblance to a seedy gas station. There were speed bumps, random people walking around for no particular reason and some of the streetlights were flickering in an ostensible attempt to burn out altogether. Annabella was not afraid; she was simply not used to such surroundings. Thankfully, there was suddenly a familiar face outside the window. To Annabella's pleasant surprise, it was Brother Bryant Johnson. In the Garland's religion, any baptized male was given the title of "Brother". Annabella figured that they were just stopping by to say hello before going to their new place. "I'm glad y'all made it on time". "Evelyn just finished making dinner" he said with a friendly grin. Annabella was pretty hungry but she remembered that Sister Evelyn was not a very good cook. Her attitude was never too inviting either but Brother Johnson's warm personality made up for all that. Everyone loved him. As a teenager, he had been hit by a drunk driver and thrown thru a windshield. He had a lot of serious scars but when you got to know him, they all appeared to fade away. The Johnsons had moved from their prior residence. Their new apartment on the second floor may have been even smaller than their previous place. Annabella actually imagined fitting it inside the living room of their former home. It was not particularly neat either. Their son, Bryant Jr, was sitting in front of the television watching "Sesame Street" with two other small children. Annabella went over to say hi and was met by Evelyn. "Go ahead and sit down." Annabella did not like "Sesame Street". She hated the way Elmo and Cookie Monster used improper grammar and she had already mastered any and all content that the show had to offer. Disinterested, Annabella got up to get a glass of water. Evelyn gave Annabella a look that made her uncomfortable. "I'm kinda thirsty and I don't like Sesame Street" said Annabella. "I don't care what you like. Sit down and watch TV" Evelyn responded firmly. Annabella looked for her mother to explain or intervene but she and Brother Bryant had gone back outside. After dinner was done, Annabella went to sit back on the couch. She was getting sleepy, had school the next day and she wondered how long her mother was gonna be having "adult talk." Evelyn, Ronda and Bryant were now all in the bedroom with the door closed. Oddly, Annabella wished Joshua were there. Ronda had dropped him off to spend a couple of days with his best friend who was going to move to North Carolina later that week. Dinah was on the phone as usual and with nothing else to do, Annabella decided to listen in on what was more important than a warm bed and a good night's rest. She could hear Ronda say her dad's name a few times and things like "get away with this" and "It'll be okay." Everything else was sort of muffled and not really worth the danger of getting caught. When they finally emerged, Annabella had fallen asleep. She was awoken by Dinah and told to go get into the bed in the next room. Too tired to contest, she complied. The next morning was strange for Annabella. Her neck was stiff and she felt as if she had caught a cold or the flu overnight. As she rubbed the sleep from her eyes and sat up, she looked around to see Dinah and Ronda asleep beside her. She supposed her mother had been talking all night and was too tired or upset to leave and then unpack a bunch of items from the car. Annabella was not feeling well at all. She squeezed from in between her mother and sister and went into the bathroom. She splashed some cold water on her face and put some toothpaste on her fingertip. As she operated her makeshift toothbrush, she looked into the mirror to get a better angle. She noticed a booger and grabbed some toilet paper to blow it. She felt so much better when she got it out but that elated feeling was quickly dissipated by the sight of what materialized on her tissue. Inside of the wad was a small, brown cockroach. Annabella shrilled eerily and was sure she had awoken every occupant in the nearby housing units. Thankfully, the Johnsons had stepped out. Ronda came rushing in. “Girl, what is wrong with you?” There was a roach in my nose!” “Shhhhh! That’s not nice!” she whispered sternly. “Is it out now?” “Yeah it’s out.” I’m gonna be late for school Mama. Did you bring me some clothes up?” “You’re gonna stay home today. We have a lot of stuff to do.” Annabella was relieved. She did not feel like going to school to look at Mrs. V’s long nose and wrinkly face anyhow. She was just ready to get to their new place and get settled in. Ronda had to run some errands and the Johnsons left for work. Bryant Jr. was still sleeping. Dinah had agreed to babysit. “Nah-Nah’ wake up!” Annabella said with a shake. “There was a roach in my nose!” Dinah turned over and fell back asleep. Annabella sat down next to her. Did no one think this was as gross as Annabella did? Annabella had seen roaches before. There had even been some big, flying ones in their house that sent her and her siblings running across a room or two but this one was tiny and whenever Annabella had seen a small one in someone’s house, it always meant that there were many, many more in accompaniment. She got goosebumps at the very thought and as she went to ease her chills of disgust by rubbing her arms, there was another six-legged friend there to greet her. Annabella jumped out of the bed and went to the living room. She began to actually watch for them which only gave her more of the creeps. She just wanted to go back home. Once she collected herself, she called her dad at his office.

William worked in the restoration of antique homes. Floods and hurricanes often destroyed them in their city. Therefore, it was quite the lucrative business. William was the best in New Orleans and had helped teach the trade to family members along with anyone who had the talent and the willingness to learn. He even adopted a program to help underprivileged individuals and ex-convicts become skilled at the trade. He had a giant office with his name in colossal gold letters adorned at the building's summit. William, or "Bill" as everyone referred to him, had gained even more popularity in the early 80's after a horrid occurrence ended up being published in the city's main newspaper.

One night, while driving home from grocery shopping, William and Ronda were pulled over by a police officer's vehicle. When the policeman initially flashed his lights, there was no safe place to pull the truck over and being that it was getting pretty late, William was somewhat wary of doing so. Just as William was pulling over to the shoulder, the officer rammed the back of his vehicle. Though William was a well-educated, successful African American male, he knew that there were rules that needed to be followed whether or not personal feelings or pride were involved. Had Ronda not been with him, things would have probably transpired differently. "Just relax baby and don't say anything unless you have to" William told Ronda. Officer Macintosh stepped out of his vehicle with his hand on his firearm. He walked over to Ronda's side of the car first. "What is the problem?" she asked agitatedly. "Your boyfriend here didn't heed my sirens." He's my husband and if you would've given us a chance..." "I really didn't ask you to speak Ma'am, now won't you gone ahead and step out of the vehicle for me." As the petite woman began to step out of the truck, she said, "I don't understand why I have to get out." "Alright! Go 'head and stay in!" Macintosh slammed the door only to catch her leg that was still in it. She yelped in pain, "What the fuck is your problem?!" William yelled. Officer Macintosh ran over to William's side and drew his weapon on William. "Oh, the boy got some spunk!" Macintosh grabbed his radio and called for back up. "Step out of the car now!" William looked and nodded at Ronda to let her know to stay calm. William got out with his hands up. Macintosh cuffed William and whispered "You should've instructed the little woman to do what she's told. I sure am sorry about those sexy, little brown legs though. I guess I'll have to massage em later on." William couldn't contain his anger and began to shuffle around. Macintosh could feel William's fury radiating through his body. Enraged at his audaciousness, Macintosh punched William across the face. He pulled out his nightstick and began to beat William across the back and head. William saw Ronda get out and screamed for her to get back in. Backup arrived and the newly involved officers immediately jumped to the aid of Officer Macintosh. Somehow, the handcuffs came undone and William became engulfed in a full-fledged brawl. Given his background as a championship prizefighter, he gave the police a fairly reasonable yearning to use deadly force. Hearing Ronda's screams and seeing the neighbors come from their houses may have been the only thing that saved his life that night. William Jr., who had been staying over at Ronda and William's house, heard the commotion down the street and ran outside to see what was going on. The nineteen-year-old young man ran into the melee to his father's defense and was also beaten. Eventually, by several officers, William was subdued and taken into custody. One of the other officers told Ronda to go home. William, Jr. and Ronda all filed lawsuits and won a total of $4,000,000 in damages against the police department and the state of Louisiana. William received the majority of the compensation thanks to one candid policeman witnessing the brutality accompanied by the fact that Macintosh had been out of his jurisdiction all along. The settlement helped to heighten the success of William's company, making it more productive than ever before. William had a sense of vindication from that moment onward. He and Ronda were doing pretty good. They took a trip to Acapulco and the kids had everything they wanted and needed. William was happy. The Garlands were officially on top after that, and it felt good. It felt damn good.

William was glad to hear from Annabella. He knew that she was still upset about the entire ordeal and he wanted to make sure she was handling things decently. "Daddy, why do I have to stay here?" "This place is gross and Sister Johnson is being so weird!" "Okay now, don't be rude." "I'm sorry, but I don't want to be here." "Baby girl, I have no idea why you're there. You'd have to ask your mother but you can come stay with me any time you want to. Plus, I'm gonna have a surprise for you real soon!" "A surprise? Tell me! Tell me!" "I have to call you back later Belly, I have a client coming in." "OK, bye" Annabella said with a sigh.

Annabella's hopes of moving to a new place didn't happen nearly as soon as she had hoped. By the skin of her teeth, Dinah was graduating high school and getting ready for prom. Prom was normally not an option for the Garlands due to their religion. Their creed held the belief that such dances were "of the world", led to promiscuity and had no place within their religious community's social events. This was deemed unfair by the youngsters considering Jehovah's Witnesses never had any church-based gatherings for children and teens at all. While Annabella agreed that this tradition was complete nonsense, she wondered why all of their practices and beliefs were suddenly going so quickly down the drain. They had not changed their religion but they were attending services a lot more infrequently. Perhaps this was because of Ronda's depression. Or it could have been related to the manner in which Jehovah's Witness families were treated when they made the choice to dissolve a marriage. The family was made to sit in the back of the Kingdom Hall and no one there was allowed to talk to them regarding anything separate from Bible scriptures. Even friends that had come over to their house for parties, left their kids there to be babysat, and even borrowed or been given money during their own hard times, shunned the Garlands as if they had never met. The children of the divorced couples were also not allowed to be associated with although they had nothing whatsoever to do with the choices and actions of the parents. Annabella was heartbroken by this and pledged that as an adult, she would never be linked to such an alienating, two-faced organization of people.

It turned out that Sister Johnson was somewhat of a seamstress and she agreed to make Dinah's dress. Annabella was happy for Dinah and felt that no girl should miss her high school prom. She wondered what William would think of all this though. Joshua was already back and the small, two-bedroom apartment was becoming stuffy and crowded. Ronda had a close friend that said they could come and stay with her for a little while. Her place was not fancy, but it was much neater and roomier. Sandy was a very nice lady. She was also a member of the congregation. However, she had been having some issues and didn't attend meetings at the Hall as frequently as the Garlands once had. Annabella and Dinah spent most of their time at Sandy's while going back to the Johnson's place once in a while. Joshua had been staying on and off at William's condo but he was becoming very defiant and would often run away to wherever his mother and sisters were staying. This was particularly the case when he no longer wanted to follow William's rules. William believed in "spare the rod, spoil the child" which led to accusations of abuse as well as constant coddling of Joshua by way of Ronda's often nonsensical thoughts and actions. This dynamic became confusing because when Ronda and William were still under one roof, she would encourage physical discipline of the children. Annabella even remembered her siblings getting into trouble at school and hearing Ronda shout, "Let the beating commence!" when William pulled into the driveway. Now, Ronda's selective memory was in full effect.

Joshua and William never saw eye to eye on much. William bought Joshua every video game and new pair of sneakers he ever asked for but William always wished that Joshua would be more interested in outdoor activities like fishing and sports. William tried persuading and sometimes even verbally insisting that Joshua come along on fishing trips with Joshua's older brother William Jr. but Joshua always managed to either get out of it or make it miserable for everyone else by moping throughout the outing. William chalked it up to Joshua simply being a computer nerd and was hopeful that he'd do great things with that brain of his one day.

Early one evening, while at Sandy's, Annabella sat up and began thinking of the whirlwind that was now her life. She went from having everything she ever needed and wanted, to living practically out of a box. She still had no answers as to why this had all happened or whether it would go on for an eternity. She didn't want her parents to get back together like most eight-year-olds would have though. She just wanted them to act as if they had ever cared about one another at all in the first place.

Annabella remembered the story of her parents getting together. Ronda worked as a clerk on the Ft. Landon Army Base. She would check items in and out for the soldiers and officers. William would come in making jokes and being boisterous. He was always the center of attention. Ronda did not like William one bit at first but she began to see the charm and potential in him in a very short time. William was moving pretty far up the ranks which was very uncommon in the '60s and '70s. Ronda was already in a committed relationship with a man named Todd. Todd was a short-statured gentleman with a sensitive spirit. Ronda loved him very much. He made her feel the way she felt she deserved. Ronda had dated other men and preferred them to be older. She had gone on many dates but no one made her feel like Todd did. William, on the other hand, being charming, strong and handsome, made her work just as hard to be with him. He knew his worth and refused to simply settle. This intrigued Ronda and she began to fall for him despite his currently committed union to his wife Mallory. William had brought his son William Jr. on the base and Ronda thought he was the most adorable little boy she had ever seen. He had a head full of thick, curly hair and the chubbiest cheeks. "Oh my goodness; what a cutie!" said Ronda. "He's handsome like his daddy. Ain't he?" said William. Ronda rolled her eyes. "I've been trying to find somebody to watch him." "His mama had to take his sister Anastasia to visit their Aunt and he has to stay and go to his doctor's appointment." "I'll watch him for you. How could I say no to a face like that?"

Ronda said with a smile. After work, William went to pick Jr. up from Ronda's barracks. Immediately upon opening the door, William stared down at Ronda's thighs. "She sure has nice legs for a short little thing" he thought. It wasn't hard to notice with the teeny-weeny shorts she was wearing. "Did you have fun with Ms. Ronda?" "Yes Daddy! She's so nice!" Ronda blushed at the look of approval they both gave her. "I might need you to watch him again sometime if you can" said William. "I'll think about it" she said with a wink. After that, William's visits to Ronda's place became more and more commonplace, oftentimes, without William Jr. One night, Ronda had on fewer clothes than ever. William had told Ronda that while he was in Vietnam, he believed Mallory had cheated on him and that their marriage was ending. He also held some resentment toward Mallory because he believed that she was the reason his younger brother had gotten killed by the police. She accused him of stealing her necklace and he ran out of the house. He later got drunk and failed to heed an officer's commands. Mallory later found the necklace in question. Their relationship was never quite the same after that. William told Ronda that Vietnam made him a different man and how he only wanted a woman to stand by him through life-the good times as well as the bad. He seemed heartbroken and in need of compassion. Ronda could not resist or turn him away. She became putty in his hands. She couldn't deny it. She wanted him, and on a warm September night, they gave themselves to each other.

William was sewing a patch on his uniform when he was ordered to report to his superior officer at once. "Garland, what kind of bull have you gotten yourself into now!?" his Lieutenant Colonel yelled. William figured that the word had gotten out about he and Ronda's affair. He was already in the process of divorcing Mallory but it was not yet final. Ronda had gone to Colonel Dorford and told him not only about the affair but also about being four months pregnant. When she found out, she even made William sign an informal contract promising to take care of her and the baby forever. While he signed it, he never took it as seriously as Ronda apparently did. Being that William was a higher rank than she and an officer, he was considered to be fraternizing. Dorford liked Garland and considered him a fine Infantryman. Consequently, he decided to send him away to Fort McCoy, Wisconsin until he could sort things out. He was not able to say goodbye neither to Ronda nor to his wife and children before he was sent away. Ronda gave birth to Dinah thirteen days before he returned. William did everything he could to be there all to no avail. Ronda had a very difficult labor and was nearly unconscious most of the time after. Her sister Shirley had no idea what Ronda wanted her to do because she knew that Ronda had still been seeing Todd on and off before William's reassignment and that she was heartbroken with the fact that William had not yet finalized his divorce and that he had missed the birth of Dinah. She had heard rumors that he and Mallory had patched things up and that he was in fact with her during the time that Dinah was born. Considering this information, Shirley wrote Todd's name on the birth certificate and didn't think too much more of it. Upon awakening and seeing what Shirley had done, Ronda was furious. Her first thought was to try and have it rectified right away but then other thoughts came to her mind. Perhaps if she left Todd's name listed on the document, it would teach William a lesson and get him to put the pedal to the metal when it came to dissolving things with Mallory. William was never too much into paperwork and in fact, he never even took a glance at the certificate. When William saw Dinah, all he could think of was how beautiful she was. Her birth only solidified the love he possessed for Ronda. He was ready to be the man and father they both needed and deserved.

Ronda eventually got what she wanted and Mallory and William were soon divorced. Ronda was very happy although she no longer got to have fun and hang out with William anymore due to having to stay home with the baby. William loved to go out drinking, fighting and partying and Ronda wanted to him to mellow out and settle down. One night, Shirley decided to accompany William to a house party. Shirley and Ronda looked so much alike that they were often mistaken for both twins and for one another. There was even speculation that she and William had slept together during Ronda's pregnancy. Shirley loved her sister and although she found William to be very good-looking and debonair, she would have never done such a thing behind her sister's back. There was this one guy, Rodney at the party who mistook Shirley for Ronda. He had his eye on her the entire night. Strangely, this was not because of her beauty. Rather, it was because he had a vendetta against William. William had allegedly slept with his girlfriend a few years back and he was determined to get revenge. Shirley had consumed a lot of alcohol that night-much too much for a woman of her stature or for any woman at all for that matter. She decided to go lie down in one of the bedrooms. Rodney had been trying to start things all night and William was trying his best to ignore him. William and Ronda had met a couple from a church that preached about non-violence and reaching paradise on Earth and despite his rough exterior, William actually enjoyed the teachings and was interested in seeking further knowledge. Rodney figured he would have to do something drastic to get William's attention. Knowing that no man could resist a fight if his woman was involved, Rodney crept into the room and removed Shirley's skirt while she was in a drunken daze. He brought her skirt downstairs and waved it in the air. "You'll fight me now, won'tcha, chump?!" he screamed. Before William knew it, he had grabbed Rodney by the throat and threw him over the balcony onto the pavement. He ran upstairs, put Shirley over his shoulder and went back home. Being the people person that he was, everyone told the police that Rodney had too much to drink and jumped off in an attempt to show off a karate move. Rodney passed away shortly after the incident. After that night, William told Ronda that he wanted to leave the violence behind and start following a more righteous path. This decision also led him to discharge from the military and find a more family-oriented job that allowed him to at least attempt to escape the demons that were Vietnam. War wounds take a long time to heal and oftentimes, they never do.

5

WIDENING THE GAP

Annabella's stroll down memory lane made her eyes well up with tears. Ronda was now working long hours at an out of town diner and hardly ever seemed to be home. When she was, she was either too tired or irritated to do much consoling or explaining to anyone. Ronda and Annabella's relationship had gotten worse. Dinah and Joshua had taken her side and were enjoying their newfound independence and freedom while Annabella missed what they used to have and represent. She understood that there were two sides to every story and she was not about to develop hatred for a man who had been nothing but a great father to her. She loved Ronda as well but becoming and remaining close to her seemed harder than ever before.

Annabella was in one of the bedrooms at Sandy's place. Sandy's daughter Lydia was in the other room listening to music. Annabella decided to send a message to William's pager. He had a new girlfriend and when he wasn't working, he was often with her. She lived about an hour away in Baton Rouge. Annabella thought that she would not have taken her father moving on to another woman and possibly starting a new family very well but it had been nearly two years since her parents had split. Besides, Dawn was a very nice woman. Although much younger than William, she was mature enough to withstand the relationship without becoming engulfed in the drama that often followed being with an older man who was going through a messy marriage dissolution. Ronda hated the fact that Annabella liked Dawn but when Annabella was with her and William, it was the only time she felt like she had a real family again. Dawn would take her to the park, swimming, horse back riding and anywhere else she wanted to go. Annabella missed doing things with her own family so the union among William and his new love seemed to fill that void, if only for a moment. William responded to the page and called her back fairly soon. He had this happiness in his voice that Annabella was glad to hear. “Hey baby girl! How are you?” “I’m great daddy! You sound so happy!” “I am happy sweetheart!” “Do you remember I told you that I had a surprise for you?” “Yes, that was like four months ago” Annabella said with a bit of an embellished attitude. “I know, I know.” “Where are your sister and brother?” “Dinah is somewhere with her friends and Joshua is outside I think.” “Well, hurry up and go get your brother. We can ask your sister later.” “Ask her what?” Annabella asked curiously. “Just go and get your brother please” William said with a chuckle. Annabella ran downstairs to find Joshua raiding the fridge. His appetite had picked up a lot over the last year but Annabella knew that teenage boys went through all types of phases. “Joshua! Hurry up! Daddy’s on the phone.” Joshua sighed as if he were aggravated to have to walk all the way upstairs just for William to ask him a stupid question. Reluctantly, he obliged. “Hello daddy, you still there?” “Yeah I’m here. Did you get him?” “Yeah he’s here.” “Well, I was wondering if you’d like to take a little trip.” “Where?” Annabella asked excitingly. "To.........." "Daddy tell me!" "To Disney World!" Annabella was so thrilled, she dropped the phone. After picking the receiver back up to her ear she shouted, "Do you mean it?" "Now why would I say it if I didn't mean it?" William replied in a silly yet flippant tone. Annabella put the phone down to tell Joshua. "Joshua, Dad said we're going to Disney World!" "You're gonna come right?" "Hell no, I ain't going!" Joshua replied petulantly. His face looked so angry. Annabella was a bit taken aback but she was floating so high only the Lord himself would have been able to bring her back to the ground again. Annoyed with her brother's "I'm mad at the world for no particular reason" attitude, she repeated just what he had said. "Dad, he said Hell no." There were a few seconds of silence before William said, "Put him on the phone." Joshua gave Annabella a look that nearly pierced through her soul. She had no idea what was being said but she figured that Joshua was getting an earful. William was not going to force him to go on the trip but the disrespect was uncalled for and would not be tolerated. Annabella expected Joshua to be mad with her but what she did not anticipate was him hanging up, throwing the phone down and grabbing her by the neck. His grip barely allowed her to breathe but luckily, she was able to free herself from his grasp and run away. He chased her around and around through the bathroom and bedroom-connected hallway. Lydia heard all the commotion and came out of her room but even after he screamed "I'm going to fucking kill you!" she still did nothing to stop or ease his violent rampage. Annabella had never seen her brother like this before. Surely being a teen did not correlate to becoming a raving lunatic. He had teased her and even annoyed her to the point of tears before but he had never laid a hand on her. Her father had strict policies against any of his sons hitting their sisters and up to that point, her male siblings had complied. Annabella managed to get back into the bedroom and lock the door. She hurriedly called William back and told him what had happened. "I'm on my way" he responded. "Aren't you in Baton Rouge?" "I said I'm on my way." The phone went dead. Annabella was unsure how William got there so quickly but when he pulled into the parking lot and came face to face with his son, he gave him a good old fashioned, southern "butt whoopin' that sent Joshua running down the street. "If he ever hits you again, let me know" her father said as he examined the scratches on Annabella's neck. "I don't know what's gotten into that boy." "I don't know why your mother insists on not letting him live with me." William shook his head and looked at Annabella. "I'm OK daddy. Let's just get out of here soon and get to Disney World." Annabella said with a smile. "I can't wait either." he replied with a small chuckle. "You think Dinah will want to go?" he asked. "Probably not. She's been really busy lately with her boyfriend." "Well, ask her for me anyway." "I will Daddy."

One morning, Dinah, Annabella and Ronda were all sitting in the bedroom back at the Johnson's apartment. They were doing nothing in particular and they were all quite bored. Dinah nonchalantly played in Annabella's long, black hair while watching some type of talk show found on one of four channels that would appropriately play on the old television set. Thankfully, they were about to move completely very soon. Annabella couldn't take the cramped space, the vermin or the travelling back and forth between there and Sandy's place. Ronda was ironing her blouse to go to a meeting at Joshua's school. He had been getting into more and more fights. Joshua was a total nerd. He would get beaten up and get his thick bifocal glasses broken nearly once a month. As he got older, and became more interested in girls, the desire to shed his geeky image began to flourish. William thought it would only lead to trouble but he went along with Ronda's idea to nix the spectacles and decide upon contact lenses. The plan definitely was successful in heightening Joshua's confidence level but it also came with the transformational behavior of mistakenly thinking that he was now somehow a tough guy. His teenaged, scrawny body had not yet changed and all he seemed to want to do was fit in with the cool, more urban kids. After all, he had been raised in the suburbs and only recently had been exposed to a more municipal neighborhood. The kids around him noticed and were not in any hurry to let him forget it.

Suddenly, the phone rang. Dinah darted to the kitchen as fast as her short, thick legs would allow her. Annabella giggled at Dinah's face when she answered and realized that it wasn't for her. "Oh, hey Dad" she said with a pout. "Wow, I'm glad you're so happy to talk to me" he said sarcastically. "Where's Annabella?" "Hold on." "Hey Daddy!" Annabella said excitedly after Dinah handed her the phone. "Hey baby girl! I'm gonna need you to pack because we're leaving on Friday." "Really? OK. I'll do it now!" Annabella hung up without even saying goodbye or getting any further details. She ran back into the bedroom and told her mom that she needed clothes for the trip. "I don't know who your father thinks he is. I'm just supposed to jump up and pack your stuff just because he said so?" "But mom, you've known about the trip for a long time." Annabella replied. "I really don't care what I wear. I'll just pack what I have." "I don't want you going out of here looking raggedy!" Ronda replied with an increased tone to her voice. "Well, can't you just buy me some new clothes?" Annabella was confused. She had heard that her mother was going to receive child support and alimony from her father but she didn't know when or if it had begun. She had brought it up once to her mother only to be slapped and told by Ronda to "stay in a child's place." "Does it look like I have money to buy you new clothes?" Annabella remained silent and went to the corner of the room. She started to dig into the box of clothes that had not been carted away to storage units. Dinah came in from the kitchen and plopped onto the bed nearby. Annabella managed to find four suitable outfits. Given that she was currently wearing her pajamas, one of the outfits needed to be worn that day. "Can you iron this when you're done please?" Annabella asked while holding up a t-shirt and shorts. "Give me the damn clothes Annabella!" Ronda began to iron one of the shirts abruptly. "Mom, you're gonna burn..." "Shut up, shut up!" Ronda screamed. In what seemed like an instant, Ronda hit Annabella as hard as she could and perhaps out of instinct, with the iron still in her hand, she hit Annabella across the top of the head. Dinah gasped. "Mama!" Ronda stormed out of the room and into the bathroom, locking the door behind her. "Are you okay sis?" Dinah asked as she helped Annabella off the floor and onto the bed. Annabella was sobbing uncontrollably as Dinah checked her head for blood and burns. Dinah let out a sigh of relief as she realized that the iron was not on. "I must've knocked the cord from the wall when I came in." "Aren't you glad I'm so clumsy?" Dinah giggled. Annabella managed to smile through the tears. She hugged Dinah tightly. Dinah helped Annabella pack whatever they could find together.

Annabella wondered why her mother was so angry with her. She never screamed at or hit Dinah and the only time Joshua was disciplined in such a manner was when he had done something very wrong and "had it coming". Perhaps Ronda did not know how to express her sadness about everything that had happened between her and William. She could have also been hurt that her daughter was going away to Florida with her ex-husband and his new, younger girlfriend. Annabella wished that her mother would find someone. She wanted her mother to be happy. However, Annabella was beginning to grow numb to Ronda taking out her frustrations on her simply because Annabella loved her father and wanted to spend as much time with him as she could outside of the every- other-weekend visitation that the courts had assigned. Annabella actually wanted to live with her father. During court, the judge had asked Annabella whom she wished to reside with. She had no idea what to say. She had so much fun when she was with her dad but she knew if she said she wanted to live with him permanently, her mother would never forgive her. The last thing Annabella wanted to do was cause her mother to be upset and essentially, make things worse between the two of them.

Disney World was amazing! It was better than Annabella could have ever dreamed. William was enjoying himself too and was acting like a silly, giant kid. Dawn was great and allowed Annabella and William to bond without attempting to steal all his attention. They rode every ride, watched every show, did nearly all the activities and ate to their heart's desire. Annabella tried lobster for the first time and fell head over heels. Unfortunately, the same thing happened in the restroom from her eating too much of it. Annabella didn't care though. She was having the time of her life and for once in a long, long time, she had no worries. She was happy again. After Disney World, William suggested that Annabella stay with Dawn in Baton Rouge until things died down concerning Ronda and Annabella's incident prior to the trip. Annabella didn't mind this in the least. Dawn was almost like having another big sister. She taught Annabella how to make peanut butter cups and chocolate covered cherries from scratch. She even let her watch TV all night. She was having a great summer. When Ronda told William that he'd better bring her back, Annabella's heart sank. She knew that Ronda was going to have a lot of questions as she always did when Annabella would return from a visit with her father. She didn't even seem to miss Annabella and would only engage in conversations that involved some type of scrutiny or interrogation. Despite Annabella's reluctance, there was a silver lining around having to go back. Ronda had finally gotten them their own place. It was a two-bedroom townhouse right across from Sandy's unit. The neighborhood was not what many would find suitable for young children and while Annabella didn't have a room to call her own, she was simply happy to no longer have to share a place with another family, especially one containing Evelyn Johnson.

Ronda and William continued to bicker their way through divorce proceedings. Annabella didn't know what was taking so long. The divorce had been final for nearly two years. Yet, Ronda always found issues with their previous monetary deals and insisted on going back to court frequently. Annabella just wanted all the fighting to stop. It had gotten so bad that the judge had ordered the family to go to counseling. Dinah and Joshua refused to participate. That left Annabella, her mom, and her dad to try and hash things out. During one session, the therapist gave Annabella a diary to write in. Ronda and William argued during all five court-assigned sessions and just as Annabella suspected, things only got worse.

Annabella was getting tired of playing within the brick enclosure that her mother would not let her ride her bike outside of due to the dangers of the neighborhood. She spent most of her time playing with Sandy's five-year-old son. Although Sandy and her children were like family to the Garlands, Annabella was ten years old and wanted to play with children her own age. Summer was almost over and she was hoping to start a fresh year with new beginnings. As time went on, Annabella realized that she had a knack for writing. She began to write poems to express her feelings and her journal entries were quite passionate and vivid for a girl her age. Annabella had not seen her father since the last visitation weekend. Annabella loved her time with William but she hated the manner in which they occurred. Because Ronda and William couldn't stop fighting with one another, the judge ordered them to meet at a communal place in order to "exchange the child" as he put it. The chosen spot was a nearby fast-food restaurant. This was not only hurtful to Annabella, it was also embarrassing. It began to affect Annabella so much that she not only didn't want to see food from that restaurant, she began to not want to eat food altogether. By this time, William and Dawn had decided to end their relationship. William had said that it was because she was simply too young for him but Annabella believed that it may have been due to him not being quite ready to settle down so quickly after such a long marriage. He was now seeing two women, one named Laurie and one that Annabella had yet to meet.

William had to skip one of his weekends with Annabella because he had to go out of town on business. While she understood and he promised to make it up to her, she still missed him terribly which caused her to doodle the words "I miss you daddy" in her diary. It was a very hot day outside and the air conditioning was not blowing out cold air as strongly as it should have. The manager would either forget to put in the work order for repairs or he simply couldn't be bothered with it to do so in a prompt manner. Annabella decided to take a cool shower to at least somewhat combat the heat if even for a short while. Mid-shower, Annabella heard a ruckus going on outside the door. Initially, she was afraid to come out. She was home alone and did not want to be met with any burglars or murderers upon her exit from the bathroom. She put her ear to the door to see if she could hear a voice of some sort. It was Ronda. She was rambling on about something but it also sounded like she was in a fight with someone. Annabella put her bathrobe on and opened the door to see her mother throwing things around the bedroom.

Ronda was throwing clothes and some of Annabella's other items into bags and boxes. "Mom what are you doing?" "You miss him so much, why don't you go live with him then!?!" Ronda screamed. Annabella glanced over to the bed and realized that she had left her journal open where she had scribbled about missing her father. What she didn't grasp was why Ronda was so angry. "You got what you wanted William! Come and get her!" Ronda shouted through the phone receiver. Annabella could hear her father yell something back but she was unsure what he had said. Ronda ran downstairs dragging Annabella's belongings behind her and sat them next to the front door. She returned back upstairs and slammed the door to her bedroom. Annabella waited outside for William who had just arrived back in town. He got there within twenty minutes. "Daddy, I only wrote that I miss you in my book and she just got crazy!" "I'm going to go in and talk to her" said William. "I don't think you should do that." Annabella said almost pleadingly. "It'll be okay. You stay here." William went upstairs and opened the door. "Ronda, what the hell is going on? I was with a client and you pull this?" "I'm tired of that girl always putting you on some type of pedestal." "I'm her parent too!" Ronda said as she began to tear up. "She loves you and you know it; you just have to stop being so rough with her. She's going through a lot." "*She's* going through a lot? What about *me*? You left *me*! Ronda screamed. "I've done everything I can for you. I don't even know why you have the kids living here. No wonder she always wants to come with me!" said William. "Get out of my God damn house! Get out!" Ronda shouted. "You see? This is why we couldn't have ever stayed together." Annabella who had been listening to the entire conversation, ran downstairs as fast as she could and pretended as if she were simply getting a glass of water. "Let's go baby girl." William called his girlfriend Laurie and told her that Annabella would be coming to stay for a while. She didn't hesitate whatsoever and welcomed Annabella with open arms. Laurie had a nice house. She worked for an investment firm and did quite well for herself. She had an eight-year-old son named Blake. His father had died a few years back and it was just him and Laurie. Blake loved William just like a father. Laurie and William had known each other for many years but only recently had it become romantic. Annabella and Blake hit it off immediately and Blake always thought she was pretty cool "for a girl". On the weekends, Laurie would always make them extra cheesy nachos and let them watch movies and play video games all night. Annabella hated the fact that her father worked so much but she understood that he was in high demand and that he needed to do what was necessary to provide for the family. One night, he came in after Laurie and Blake had long been asleep. Annabella asked him, "Dad why doesn't Mom have a nice place like this? You don't pay child support and alimony?" "What do you know about that stuff sweetie?" "Come on Daddy, I'm not a dumb kid. Plus, I've heard it in court and I've heard Mom talk about it a lot." "Yes, baby girl, I pay your mom child support and alimony." "How much?" asked Annabella. William gave her a look as if to indicate that he was shocked by her boldness. "I just want to know because she always says that she doesn't have any money and if you are giving her some and she has a job, that doesn't make any sense." "Annabella, I really don't think..." "Just tell me pleeeaasse." Annabella begged. "I'm not going to do that" William replied. "You'll find all that out in due time. Now go to bed." Annabella felt that she was smart enough and mature enough to understand these types of things. She knew something wasn't right. If her Dad was giving her mother money, why was she still so angry and why were they living in such a bad neighborhood? Annabella knew that her father was not the type of man to not take care of his children. Something was definitely wrong and Annabella was going to find out exactly what it was.

After about three weeks at Laurie's, Ronda called William and said that Annabella could come home if she wanted to. Annabella wanted to stay with her father but she missed Dinah and despite what Joshua had done to her in the past, she wanted to see him as well. She could never stay mad at him for some reason. She wondered if it was because they looked so much alike and had the same sense of humor. Dinah was awesome but she always seemed to be the more sensitive of the bunch. Annabella and Joshua would tease each other all the time about one another's looks. Joshua would call Annabella "Bucky Beaver" because of her large front teeth and Annabella would make fun of his skinny body and misshapen head. He could no longer refer to her as 'Jelly Belly' though. She had shed all her baby weight and was actually quite thin. This may have been due to her problem with food regarding the fast-food exchange but nonetheless, she was happy to have the extra weight off. Her return to a normal healthy lifestyle was brought on by Laurie's good observational skills accompanied by her good cooking. Laurie had noticed that Annabella did not look well and that she had not been eating much, not even on 'Nacho Fridays'. Reluctant to break the bond and trust that she had developed with Annabella, Laurie told William anyway. That same night, he told Laurie to prepare Annabella a plate of the food she had cooked- steak, mashed potatoes and broccoli. Laurie sat the plate in front of Annabella. It looked so delicious but Annabella didn't want it. She felt as if she had no control over what was going on with her family and her refusing to eat was the only thing that she had any power over. At least that's what she thought. "I want you to eat every bit of it or we're gonna have a serious problem and I mean it" William said sternly. Annabella stared at the plate and figured out what she had been doing to herself. She knew that no matter what she did, her family would never be the same and she just had to learn to accept it. Annabella ate every bite and it was delicious. Annabella respected her father very much but she was not afraid of him. In all of her life, he had only spanked her four times and usually with what Annabella felt was good reason. He did however, lose his temper sometimes and periodically seemed to forget his own physical strength.

When Annabella was about six years old, William once slapped her face so hard that it left a handprint. The house the Garlands lived in during this time was William's and Ronda's first large home. In the very late '80s, William was given a house by one of his clients. It was almost like two houses in one. There was one kitchen and one living room on both the first and second floor, five bedrooms, a grand dining room, a huge backyard and an indoor, pool-sized swim spa. Everyone except for Ronda adored the house. Olivia Patterson had been so grateful for all William had done for her, she felt it was the least she could do to exhibit her appreciation. Despite Mrs. Patterson's and her husband's success, their children at eighteen and twenty years of age, were not fortunate enough to be supplied with the capabilities of overcoming the temptations of the world. Olivia's son was a recovering alcoholic and drug addict and spent most of his time alone, avoiding the world. Her daughter Penelope, on the other hand was much more free-spirited. She was a very pretty, intelligent young lady but she always seemed to want to hang with the local riff raff despite Olivia's constant disapproving protests. Olivia was a recovering addict herself and she knew that one day, her daughter's compulsions would lead her down a path all too grim to possibly see the light of day again. One night, Penelope stole Olivia's van. It was not uncommon for her to do such a thing and initially, Olivia didn't think much of it. Unfortunately, this time, she didn't return days later in the high, inebriated stupor as she usually did. Olivia had called the police but the most they could do was file a missing person's report and hope for the best. Considering the fact that she was an adult, they did not search for her and informed Olivia that their hands were tied. Olivia was devastated and feared the worst had happened. She sulked into William's office, plopped into the chair and began to sob. "Still no word from Penny?" William asked. "I just don't know what to do Bill, what if she's de....?" "Let's not think like that, I'll do what I can to help you find her. I'm sure she's alright." About four days after his and Olivia's meeting, William was at the gas station filling up his truck. A tattered, scrawny man walked up to him and asked for change. William hated dopeheads and beggars but instead of reacting in his normal, enraged, "get the hell away from me before I hurt you" manner, something clicked. He thought maybe this junkie might know where to find Penelope. He bought the guy a pint of whiskey, gave him twenty bucks and added a little intimidation to help him spill the beans. The man didn't seem to be too credible but he did give William a street name that was not too far away with a house where a lot of drug activity, namely heroin, was being sold and used. William was tired and just wanted to go home and rest but it was Friday night and he thought it'd be a perfect time to find a bunch of druggies enjoying their weekend. He told the guy to walk and he'd follow him to the house. He was not about to allow a junkie to ride in his automobile and stink up his upholstery. The man went inside and came back out about twenty minutes later. "There's a girl in there but I don't know what her name is. She don't look too good though bro." The man walked away and seemed to disappear into the shadows. William wasn't sure what he'd find but he knew he had to try. He began to look around the street for Olivia's van but it was nowhere in sight. "She probably exchanged it for drugs" William thought. He could hear the music blasting from the place and knew that they would never be able to hear a knock at the door. Besides, he didn't want those inside to have a chance to conceal themselves or their drugs. He barged in and began looking in and around each corner of the filth-ridden residence. "Penelope!....Penelope! You in here sweetie?" The people inside looked like zombies seemingly unaware that they were being intruded upon. William internally thanked God that none of these lost souls were his kids. William hated drugs and always believed that only weak people indulged in them. He did however, love his alcohol. To him, nothing was better than having a glass of Crown Royal after dinner or an ice-cold beer with a couple dozen oysters. Just as he was about to give up hope in finding Penelope, he heard a thud-like sound coming from the bathroom. He knocked but when there was no answer, he broke down the door. There, in the middle of the floor, pale as a ghost, was Penelope. Her frail body just laid there as if she were a corpse. William grabbed her, put her into the bathtub and turned on the cold water. He began to slap her cheeks and shout her name as loud as he could. "Penny! It's Bill, don't leave me, come on!" She barely moved her head from one side to the other but that's all he needed. She was alive. He wrapped her in his jacket and carried her to his truck. Rather than take her to a hospital, he drove her straight home to her parents. William rushed in and laid her on the couch. Olivia began to bawl and kiss her daughter all over her face. Thinking the family needed to be alone, William crept out while all the attention was on Penelope.

Three weeks later, Olivia showed up at his office with good news regarding Penelope's recovery as well as the keys to one of her four properties. She later met up with him at the house to show him around and to discuss the arrangements. She wanted to assure William that there were absolutely no strings attached and that the house was now one hundred percent his property.

Annabella went with him to look at the house. She was so excited to see the indoor pool and what would be her new bedroom. After taking a tour, they all sat down in the downstairs living room. They began discussing the elements of the home and other grown up stuff that Annabella didn't too much care about nor quite comprehend. She did, however, overhear William tell Olivia that he would meet up with her on the following Thursday to go over details about some work that he was to do on another one of her homes. Annabella interrupted "Daddy you can't do it *this* Thursday because you promised to take me to the zoo!" "I can take you to the zoo another day baby" he replied with a stern tone that seemed to imply annoyance with Annabella's interrupting outburst. Annabella was big on promises. She figured if someone were willing to verbally swear or promise to do something, they'd be more likely to carry out the action. That was the first time that William had ever broken a promise to her. She was dumbfounded. So much in fact that she said the first words that came to mind "You're a liar!" she shouted. Immediately, she wished she had kept those words in her throat and that she could just disappear into oblivion. "Come here right now! William yelled. Annabella walked over to him slowly. The slap seemed to echo throughout the house. "Don't you ever call me a liar!" Annabella clutched her cheek in shock. She looked at her father with tears and disbelief in her eyes and ran to the bathroom in order to avoid making a bigger scene in front of Olivia. "Should I leave?" she exclaimed. "No. She'll be alright" said William. Annabella stayed in the bathroom for what seemed like forever. William knocked lightly. "Annabella, come out of there." "I don't wanna see you" said Annabella still sobbing. "Open it now Belly." Thinking that she may make things worse by not complying, she apprehensively opened the door and stepped out with her arms folded. "First of all, unfold your arms when I'm talking to you." "Secondly, I am not going to apologize for hitting you because you deserved it but I didn't mean to hit you that hard." He began to inspect her face and then went to the kitchen to make Annabella an ice pack to ease the redness and aid in getting rid of the plain as day handprint embedded in her cheek.

William hugged her tightly and soon after, all was well again between them.

Dinah loved the house-especially how spacious it was. She liked not having her parents breathing down her neck every five minutes. There were a lot of places for a teenaged girl to disappear and sneak in late-night phone calls, or merely just have some alone time. Despite Dinah's obvious adolescent angst, Annabella and Dinah were extremely close and per usual, Annabella could sense that something was bothering or different about her sister. Dinah loved to cook and more than that, she loved to eat. Annabella thought it would be fun if they had a "girls' night". They'd make their favorite seafood nachos, watch movies and pig out on candy, soda and other horrible foods. Dinah thought it would be a great idea to invite Lizette. Lizette was the daughter of a couple within their congregation. Other kids within the spiritual circle were the only acquaintances or friends the Garland children were able to socialize with. Annabella really wanted the girls' night to be with just herself and Dinah but Lizette was really funny and cool so Annabella agreed to include her in the night's festivities. Lizette was a bit of a tomboy. She wore baggy clothes and she never seemed interested in anything girly like makeup or hairstyles. She would also sometimes burp very loudly and follow it with a description of what she'd eaten minutes before. Annabella liked Lizette's carefree personality and she could certainly see why she and Dinah were so close.

Lizette finally arrived and the night was going great. Dinah was smiling from ear to ear and they were all laughing, watching music videos, dancing and having a good time. They all decided to make palettes on the upstairs living room floor. The night was winding down and Annabella was getting a bit tired. "Why don't you go get in my bed so you can stretch out and be comfy?" Dinah asked, turning toward Annabella. "Me and Lizzie will sleep in here so we won't bother you." "But I wanna stay in here with you guys!" Annabella said with a pronounced pouty lip. "Okay but you need to go to sleep because Mom will probably get mad if you stay up too late." Annabella knew that her sister only wanted big girl time with her friend and because she was trying to cheer her sister up, she turned over and pretended to sleep. After about an hour or so, Annabella actually began to fall sleep and was nodding off. She overheard Dinah and Lizette giggling and talking about cherries and whipped cream. Annabella hoped they weren't going to have sundaes without her but she was too tired from all the excitement. Annabella had a bit of a bedwetting problem. She had to get up frequently so that she didn't have accidents and Annabella didn't want to embarrass Dinah nor herself so despite her being super sleepy and comfortable, she managed to groggily open her eyes. She looked over at the TV and her young mind went into a state of confusion. There was a man and two women on the screen and they were naked and laying on a big black bed by a swimming pool. The man and woman were licking whipped cream and cherries off of the other woman's breast and private area. Annabella had never seen a naked man's body before and the only woman she'd ever seen naked was her mother. Annabella had never seen anyone have sex. She wasn't even sure if what she had just witnessed was indeed sex. Annabella noticed the VCR light was on so it must have been a tape. "Lizette must have brought it over" thought Annabella. She knew that Dinah would have never risked keeping a tape like that in the house, especially with parents like William and Ronda. Annabella started hearing smacking noises coming from the other side of the living room floor where Dinah and Lizette were sleeping. They were both under the blankets together. Annabella gasped and pulled her head under the covers. She had no idea if they heard her or not but she didn't make another sound. Unfortunately, Annabella never got to make her trip to the restroom.

The place was great for throwing parties. The Garlands' best friends, James and Mindy Spedman came over to the house while William and Ronda were out to talk to Dinah and Annabella about their plans to throw the couple a shindig for their Anniversary that was about four months away. An anniversary was the only holiday that individuals of their faith were allowed to celebrate or participate in. Mindy and James were so much fun to hang out with and despite their strong support of the religion, they both loved to drink and have fun. Mindy was a free spirit. She wore bright colors and always seemed to be the life of the party. The spunky side of her personality was another element that made her such a joy to be around. One night, the two families decided to go out for a night on the town. Although all the kids were tagging along, the adults still insisted upon hitting up Bourbon Street. Sometimes, there weren't too many rowdy people and a family could actually have a safe, enjoyable time. After having dinner and listening to some live bands, it had gotten pretty late. The kids seemed to be all tuckered out and ready to call it a night. Before leaving, Annabella needed to use the restroom. Mindy and Annabella were already holding hands so she agreed to take her. There weren't many suitable establishments on that street to do so, especially for a six-year-old girl. Finally, they found a decent enough place and walked in. It was not only a bar but it was also a restaurant and looked as if the bathrooms would likely be moderately clean. There was an older White woman working behind the bar. She had her back towards them and she was cleaning the counters. “Two drink minimum!” she yelled without turning to face the pair. “My niece just needs to use the restroom. I’ll buy two drinks though.” The woman turned to them with her grin immediately shifting to a scowl. “She can’t use it.” “Is it broken or something?” Mindy asked. “Nope!” “I just have the right to say who can and can’t use it” the woman said snidely. Giving the woman a cynical “okay”, Mindy put her hand on Annabella’s shoulder and began to escort her out. Upon their exit, she heard the woman attempt to whisper to a customer, “I don’t want no damn niglet piss on my toilet seat anyway.” Mindy stopped in her tracks but thought of Annabella and decided to continue with the departure. Annabella could no longer hold her urine and before reaching the rest of the family already at the cars, she ended up having an accident. This only angered Mindy more. She told William, Ronda and James what had happened but she and William were the only ones who had not had a few too many that night. They decided to go back and confront the woman leaving James and Ronda with the kids. Mindy walked in first. The woman immediately sensed trouble and nodded at two men to go toward her. This was William’s cue to walk in instantly exhibiting the many inches and pounds he had on both of them. Looking intimidated, they did nothing at that moment but remain standing. Mindy slammed down twenty dollars and said, “Give me four shots of Jack!” “We’re fresh out” the barkeep responded. Mindy immediately jumped over the bar exhibiting a move similar to something found in a typical Kung Fu film and grabbed the bottle of Jack Daniels. As the woman tried to grab her, Mindy held up the bottle threatening to strike the woman. The bouncers ran towards Mindy only to be stopped in their tracks by William with two grips around their necks, shoving them forcefully to the floor. Both men hobbled outside. Mindy poured four shots of the liquor for her and William. She then made her way to the bathroom and made sure to leave a couple of "trickles" for the *nice lady* at the bar. Upon exiting, Mindy exclaimed, "I made a little bit of an oopsie so you might wanna get back there and clean it up sweetie." She and William then walked swiftly back to their cars and got outta there as quickly as they could. Annabella overheard them telling the story a few days later and although she was told to never display such behavior, she was happy that Mindy stood up for her. Ronda pretended to be disgusted at their behavior but deep down she wished that it had been her and William instead. Ronda was no gentle flower but she loved to give off the façade that her level of class was insurmountable.

Annabella adored Mindy. She didn't think of her as a friend of the family but simply as family. Although Annabella loved her mother, secretly Annabella sometimes wished that Mindy were her mom instead. This was especially the case when Ronda would scold or whoop her for oftentimes very petty reasons. Mindy just exuded so much life and gave off a certain luminosity that was palpably absent from Ronda's spirit. Annabella knew that Ronda sensed this and rather than attempting to alter the way she presented herself as a person and mother, Ronda chose to show resentment toward her young daughter.

Whenever Annabella had a loose tooth, William would pull it out for her. It had become sort of a traditional, bonding experience for them and although Annabella would be scared, she grew to treasure those moments. After picking Annabella up from school, Ronda would often take her over to William's place of business so she could finish up some "paperwork" before heading home. Dinah and Joshua would usually already be at home by this time considering their school day ended about an hour prior to Annabella's. The workday at William's office was coming to an end so Annabella went to her father and told him that her tooth was ready to come out. "I'll pull it out when we get home" said William. "But look Daddy!" "It's hanging!" William took a closer look and saw that it was indeed ready to come out at that moment. He also remembered that Annabella nearly choked during a previous attempt to procrastinate the removal of a hanging incisor. "Okay, okay go get the stuff." Annabella ran to the office kitchen and grabbed a small cup and the salt from the cupboard. She filled the cup halfway with water, mixed in the salt and quickly heated the concoction in the microwave. She then scurried back to her father. William always jokingly pretended as if he were a doctor and made the experience very elaborate. While this helped to put Annabella's mind somewhat at ease, she nonetheless began to feel that nervous feeling. "I'm scared Daddy." Mindy who had been working in the front office for some extra cash was putting away some files and overheard Annabella's apprehension. Making funny faces to make Annabella laugh, Mindy walked over to comfort Annabella only to be cut off by Ronda. "I'll hold her hand so you can go finish your work." "But Mama, I want Auntie Mindy to do it." Ronda gave Annabella a cold stare and immediately dropped her hand in an abrupt manner that sent it swinging to and fro. Back at home, Ronda chose not to acknowledge Annabella at all and even told Dinah to fix Annabella's dinner since according to Ronda, Annabella probably thought Dinah was a better cook than Ronda was anyhow. This type of envy was quite common where Ronda was concerned and after that day, the disdain for her once closest friend Mindy, began to grow like a weed.

Mindy had to go out of town due to a death in the family

and during her absence, William had hired Ilene, a friend of a friend to do some temp work. Ilene, although a very nice lady, often exhibited signs and actions of absentmindedness. She would get staff lunch orders completely wrong, incorrectly take messages and altogether forget basic tasks. She had misplaced a very crucial file containing an invoice for one of William's biggest clients who had begun to try and stiff him out of some of the money he was owed for his services. Mindy had come back and was helping him look for it. She and Ronda had torn the office upside down that Friday because they were closed on weekends and they'd have plenty of time to get things back in order by the time the work week started back up again. Ronda began to become frustrated and believed that Mindy was the one who really lost the file and that the only reason that it was being blamed on Ilene was because it was Ronda's idea that they hire her as a temporary secretary in the first place. William had grown tired of the type of hints that Ronda was beginning to drop about the supposed reasoning behind so many late nights and the amount of "help" that William seemed to need from Mindy over the last few weeks. "I can't believe you could misplace a file like that. They're one of our biggest clients" Ronda complained. "Girl, you know I wasn't even here when that happened." "You always seem to be here on every other occasion now don't you?" "I really don't need this right now Ronda." "Well there's the door. You're quite welcomed to go through it" Ronda said nastily while pointing to the entryway. Mindy let out a quick sigh and thought it might be best if she go to the kitchen to put on some more coffee. Perhaps everyone was just tired and needed a little 'pick me up' after having already spent nearly four hours looking for the lost file all to no avail. Mindy was sipping a glass of water while she waited for the coffee to finish.

Ronda walked in and attempted to start making coffee. "I'm already making a pot." "You just seem to have it all figured out huh?" Ronda was growing increasingly angry at Mindy always being at the office. She also didn't like the fact that Mindy and William had such a good rapport and friendship and would often laugh and make jokes that Ronda either didn't get or didn't think were particularly humorous. James was William's best friend and Mindy was hers so Ronda did not believe that they were having an affair. Still, something wasn't sitting right with her and she expected for Mindy to act as an employee while at work and ultimately, just stay in her place. "Look Ronda, I don't know what your problem is but I'm getting tired of you talking to me like this." "I don't give a damn what you're tired of. This is *my* business and you're not gonna disrespect me!" "Whatever Ronda" Mindy said while turning around to retrieve the finished pot of coffee. "Don't you turn your back on me bitch!" Ronda grabbed Mindy by the arm and instantly, a fight ensued. Annabella happened to be in the adjacent bathroom and overheard the racket. Mindy and Ronda were clawing at each other's faces like animals and destroying the kitchen with fists and broken glass flying. Annabella yelled for them to stop but they were going at it and never seemed to hear her. Annabella ran to get William. "Daddy! Mama and Auntie Mindy are fighting!" William jumped up and ran to the back. He immediately pulled them apart. "William, tell this bitch she's fired!" Ronda screamed. "Fired? I quit bitch!" Mindy grabbed her things from the front desk and upon her exit, she closed the glass front door with such force, it shattered all over the floor. William, with a confused look on his face asked Ronda what had happened. "You know damn well what happened! You turned my friend against me!" "Woman, what the hell are you talking about, and why is everything always my damn fault?" Ronda stormed out without giving him a response. Ronda wasn't jealous of Mindy for why most women seem to develop spiteful tendencies. After all, Mindy wasn't well off or particularly drop dead gorgeous. She simply wasn't afraid to just have a good time and be herself. That's what made Mindy beautiful and Ronda knew that no matter how hard she tried, she would never have those qualities. Mindy and Ronda later patched things up but things between them never went back to the way they once were. Although no one ever mentioned the fight again, no one ever forgot about it.

Despite the fight, Mindy and James still wanted to throw the Garlands a party for their wedding anniversary. They thought it might help get their friendship back on track and make it like it once was before. The turnout was great. Many people from the congregation showed up to celebrate the momentous occasion. The Garlands didn't have many friends outside of the congregation. This was due in large part to the fact that friends of the world or "worldly people" were considered to be bad influences and ultimately had no place in the lives of Jehovah's Witnesses. By the time the party was fully underway, many of the guests had already reached their limit or close to it in alcohol consumption. This was especially true in James' case. James loved to dance. He usually found any excuse to boogie whether it was uncalled for, silly or even blatantly inappropriate. Dinah was serving as the bartender. Although she at now fifteen years old was nowhere near close to the legal drinking age, she loved to help out and be part of the festivities. She had this aura that seemed sweet and endearing yet there was also something about her that was off-putting and made some wonder if her personality was altogether genuine. Nonetheless, Ronda adored her and thought she was the most loving and respectful of all the three children. William and Ronda arrived at their party nearly two hours late. They had been arguing all night. Ronda had accused William of flirting with the waitress who had served them that night at "Sun Dia", their favorite restaurant. They had usually requested Florence, an elderly lady to be their server but she was out with the flu. William had always been a charmer. He didn't mean anything by it. It was just his way of being friendly and welcoming. While Ronda had grown to understand and accept William's qualities, she would often take offense to his behavior and antics. This was particularly the case when the woman William was being friendly with appeared to be attractive from Ronda's perspective. This usually entailed the woman having fairer skin and long or "good hair" as Ronda and many other African Americans, namely in the South, referred to it. Ronda seemed to view these features as a threat and wholeheartedly, as the epitome of beauty. Ronda hated her brown eyes and kinky hair. She wore her green or gray colored contacts faithfully and applied chemical hair relaxer treatments every six weeks to ensure that the curls or "naps" as she called them didn't come creeping back underneath or around her straight or wavy synthetic hair. Ronda had relaxed Dinah's already thin hair and couldn't wait for the day that she could tame down the long, extreme thickness that she had to deal with on Annabella's head on a daily basis. Ronda dreaded summer vacations due to the fact that Annabella loved to swim and Ronda would always get stuck tending to her long, ferocious mane. She often ended up pawning the chore off on Dinah when she simply couldn't be bothered to deal with the motherly responsibility herself. Annabella loved her hair and it was known to receive countless compliments. However, Ronda's constant ridicule of it had a hand in diminishing Annabella's young confidence.

As the party went on and as James felt even more loose,

it became harder for him to contain himself. Mindy had gone to the kitchen to get more hors d'oeuvres but James was simply not going to wait. He grabbed Dinah and ran over to the dance floor. They began doing the two-step but when James started feeling the groove, he turned Dinah around and started dancing with her from behind. Dinah thought it was a bit inappropriate but just simply took it for what it was. William on the other hand, already angered from his and Ronda's fight, became infuriated. He grabbed James by the shirt and threw him against the wall. His feet dangled beneath his 5-foot 5-inch frame. "What the hell is your problem man?!?" William exclaimed demandingly. "Huh? Nah-uh thing man, what'd I do?" All the guests began to plead with William to let him go and he did but not before telling him to get the hell out. That was the end of the party. It was also the first and last one they ever had in that home. James later apologized and agreed not to drink so much and William agreed not to kill him. Still, the Garlands' and the Spedmans' friendships were beginning to fall apart piece by piece. Meanwhile, many other things were going along for the exact same ride.

6

PARTY POOPERS AND ROTTEN RELATIVES

One day, at the beginning of Spring Break vacation, Annabella was awoken by her mother. "Get dressed Annabella!" "Hu...huh? Why?... There's no school" Annabella said groggily while rubbing her eyes. "Do you have to argue with everything? Get dressed!" Annabella did as she was told. Annabella noticed that two of her suitcases were packed and sitting in the corner of the room. "Where are we going?" Ronda didn't respond. Annabella and Ronda got into the car. After driving for about ten minutes, Annabella began to recognize the neighborhood. She then realized that they were going to Bryant and Evelyn's place. "What are we doing here?" "Just wait in the car. I'll be right back." A few minutes passed and Ronda came back to retrieve Annabella and her suitcases. "You're gonna stay here for a few days". "Why?" Annabella asked pleadingly. "I don't have time for this Annabella." "I'll be back soon." Ronda got back into the car and drove away. She didn't even hug Annabella goodbye. Annabella stood in the driveway perplexed before reluctantly walking through the front door.

Annabella never liked staying with the Johnsons and this

was the longest time that she had ever spent with them. Evelyn had given birth to Bryant Jr. about six months prior so she spent most of her time tending to him in the middle of the night while Annabella tried to get some rest on the world's most uncomfortable Army cot in the corner of the living room of their small, two-bedroom apartment. Bryant Sr., the only member of the couple that Annabella actually enjoyed being around, worked all day and was too tired when he got home to be much good to anyone. Evelyn hardly ever cooked and would only give Annabella cold sandwiches and celery with either peanut butter or mayonnaise. Annabella missed her mom's cooking and couldn't wait for something hot to eat. Five days went by and Annabella was ecstatic. She would finally be back in her own home, eating yummy food and getting tormented by Joshua, the way it should be. Evelyn was tidying up her barely used kitchen when she got a telephone call. Annabella was busy making faces at baby BJ but managed to overhear Evelyn saying, "No problem, we could use the extra money anyway." Evelyn hung up the phone and continued to sweep the floor. "That was your mom. She said you're gonna stay with us for a couple more days." Annabella's eyes began to well up. Annabella could never rest well when she wasn't at home. As the days passed, she began to go from sentiments of sadness to moments of resentment. Evelyn was not a mean woman. She didn't seem to have many feelings at all. Annabella knew that Evelyn must have at least liked her at some point, considering the fact that she had been the flower girl at the Johnson's wedding the year prior.

Today was finally the day. Annabella had already packed all her belongings and could not have been more eager to get back home as soon as possible. She had never been so happy to see her usually indifferent mother. "Are you ready?" Ronda asked. "Yep!" "Thank you Sister Johnson!" Annabella spoke politely as she had been taught to all her life but what she really wanted to do was hightail it out of there and drive home herself at full speed. Annabella began fiddling with the radio. Evelyn had only allowed her to listen to the "Sing Praises to Jehovah" cassettes and Annabella was desperately craving something, anything with a beat. The Garlands loved music. At their previous residence, they would often have late parties and sing and dance all night. William was the biggest ham of all and loved to *hand dance*. Hand dancing is a partnership-style dance distinguished by the motions of the male's hand and received by the female's hand to follow his lead. While it was a lot of fun being his partner, there was also an element of fear connected due to William's quickness and strength. He could twirl a girl far across the room with the greatest of ease. Annabella never wanted to turn in for bed on those nights. She often wished she could've frozen those moments in time in order to one day return and relish over all the good times that would essentially make up the type of vibes she planned to have with a family of her very own someday.

Ronda seemed refreshed. She was in a much better mood and for once in a long while, her smiles lasted longer than their usual three seconds. Ronda pulled the car into a residential driveway. Annabella figured that they were just making a pit stop and was surprised to see that there were a lot of people, mainly children scattered outside. Ronda immediately began talking to her friend Candice before she shooed Annabella away urging her to mingle with the other children. Most of them were much younger than her and Annabella was not too keen on playing with babies especially after having to endure the mucous filled shrills of baby BJ for the past eight days. Annabella hated when her mom would push friendships with the younger children in the congregation. Annabella had always preferred the company of older people like Dinah or her best friend Eliza Spedman, who was around five years her senior. Annabella found a spot in the shade and just sat there waiting for Ronda to finish her rounds of socialization amid the gathering. Annabella wondered what type of party it was. The children were wearing pointed hats, there were balloons and a gaudily ugly cake atop the table adorned with other decorations and treats. "Surely this isn't a Birthday party" Annabella said to herself. Annabella had never been to a birthday party before. The reason behind it had been told to her over and over again. It had something to do with a girl requesting John the Baptist's head on a platter. Annabella always believed that the story was stupid. She did not see why one person who may or may not have actually existed, could ruin something for millions of people. Why couldn't whether or not a person's birthday would be celebrated depend solely on the attitude of that individual? Annabella asked these questions all the time and was only told to "shut up" or simply have faith and believe that everything in the Bible and the teachings of the religion were forthright in every sense of the word. If that were the case, thought Annabella, why were they now in attendance at what was now vividly clear to Annabella to be a typical, Pagan ritualized birthday party? Annabella saw Ronda sitting and schmoozing with two women that she had never seen before. "Mom do you know where the bathroom is?" Annabella asked. "Go inside, down the hall and to the right" replied Ronda without removing her eyes from her chat. Annabella stalled as long as she could in the restroom until someone knocked and twirled the doorknob in an effort to enter. Back outside, Ronda was now standing and seemed to be walking toward the exit gate. One of the women had her arms on the shoulders of a little girl wearing a pink dress with pink and white ribbons in her hair. “Denise did you thank Annabella for coming to your party?” “Thank you” the little girl said before running back to her friends. Ronda pulled out a pen and began writing on the back of a business card. “The card has my office number on it but let me give you my personal number too just in case.” Annabella by no means understood why Ronda had an office. She never seemed to be in it much and spent most of her days running household errands or attending to personal matters. “I look forward to meeting Bill on Tuesday so we can get started” said the unknown woman. Annabella began to feel ill. Sure, Ronda used swear words, scarfed down chocolate-filled eggs at Easter and King Cake during Mardi Gras, gambled from time to time and had too much to drink on some occasions but Annabella had only seen her mother break their religion’s rules in private. Publicly, she spoke adamantly against such things. Annabella had even been told that if she ever even said “Happy Birthday”, sang the song or consumed birthday cake that not only would she be punished by Ronda, but Jehovah himself would make her ill in a display of His disapproval. There was a particular instance in her Kindergarten class where Annabella ate some chocolate birthday cupcakes at school that a boy’s mother had brought in. They looked so ooey-gooey and delicious that Annabella forgot about all the prior warnings altogether. As luck would have it, Annabella got a very upset stomach and was vomiting profusely. It was likely because she had eaten four of them but when she told her mother what she’d done, Ronda insisted that Jehovah was punishing her for it. They had to go to the Kingdom Hall that night but Annabella felt much too ill. Ronda demanded that Annabella attend and claimed that Jehovah would heal her when they got there. Unfortunately, that didn't happen and Annabella vomited throughout the entire service. In fact, she was still vomiting the next day. From then on, Annabella swore she'd never eat birthday food ever again. Now, there Ronda was, plain as day, holding three slices of the presumed Devil pastry wrapped in foil. Annabella became even angrier and more confused by the second. The woman then handed Annabella a birthday hat. "I don't celebrate birthdays" said Annabella. The woman gave Annabella an odd look and looked to Ronda for clarification. With a nervous chuckle, Ronda took the hat out of Annabella's hands and put it on her head, dismissively snapping the chin strap, stinging Annabella. Giving absolutely no thought to what would later transpire, Annabella defiantly removed the hat and in a bit of an abrasive manner, put it on Ronda's head as if to imply, "you're the one who wants to celebrate birthdays all of a sudden so *you* should be the one to wear the hat!" The way Ronda looked at her daughter could've punctured the armor of the most fearless of warriors. Candice, who saw the look on Ronda's face and knew exactly what it meant, grabbed Ronda's hand, pretending to admire her new watch that was actually not so new. Removing the hat in what appeared to be in slow motion, Ronda muttered in one of the quietest tones that Annabella had ever heard her speak in. "Okay. we're gonna go now." "Annabella, apologize to your mother!" Candice yelled in an effort to sound authoritative and redirect the awkward silence and anger that had so quickly bubbled over. "Nope! It's too late, we're leaving now!" Ronda grabbed Annabella by the back of the neck and directed her both to and inside the car. It was the longest twenty-minute ride home that Annabella had ever experienced. She knew that she was going to get spanked or "whooped" as most African Americans referred to it. Ronda spoke not a word to Annabella until they were inside the empty home. "Take off your clothes and underwear and put them on the couch!" Ronda yelled. "My...underwear?" Annabella asked. "You heard what I said girl!" Hearing Ronda fumble around in William's closet, Annabella braced herself. Ronda began to walk closer to her but then made a sudden detour to the kitchen. Annabella saw this as an opportunity to apologize. "Mama, I'm sorry, I didn't mean to do that. I was jus..." "Shut up! You must have lost your damn mind but I'm about to help you find it you little witch!" Ronda held herself to a certain standard. The image of perfection fascinated her. Being the envy of all the women in the congregation gave Ronda life and she had made up her mind that nothing and no one would ever destroy what she felt she had worked so hard to obtain. Ronda turned on the faucet of the kitchen sink. She then stretched out the long, leather belt to its full span and placed it under the running water, moving it back and forth. Annabella watched in fear and confusion as she stood in the living room covered in goose bumps. "Turn around!" Ronda instructed. In tears, Annabella bent over with her hands on the arm of the couch. Annabella had been hit before but this time, when the belt touched her skin, she howled in pain. Instinctively, she put her hands across her bottom to shield the next blow. This must have angered Ronda causing the hits began to wander across other parts of Annabella's naked body. After what seemed like several minutes, Annabella felt numb and fell to the floor only to be met with a few more stinging strikes. Annabella felt as if she had fallen into a pit of giant scorpions. Her body was stinging all over. "Put your damn clothes on and get the hell out of my face and don't come out of your room until I call you!" Sobbing, Annabella ran to the couch, grabbed her clothes and then scampered to her room. Forgetting to dress, she fell face first onto her bed and screamed into her mattress until she fell asleep. Upon awakening, Annabella smelled food cooking. It was already dark out so she figured that she and Ronda would no longer be alone. Although the aroma permeating through the door cracks would normally be enticing, Annabella was not hungry nor did she wish to see or eat with her mother or anyone else for that matter. She was beginning to feel differently about Ronda but she was unsure of what to do and of what it all meant.

William was tired that night. He had just got back in town and all he wanted to do was take a shower, eat dinner, have a beer and go to bed. "It'll be ready soon" Ronda said as she stirred her red beans and sausage dish atop the stove. "How was your trip?" she asked dryly. "It was fine. I'm just tired. He replied. "How about you?" "Not so good. I had to whoop your daughter's butt a few hours ago." William knew which daughter she meant without having to ask. Ronda never hit Dinah. Then again, Dinah also never seemed to anger Ronda as much as Annabella did. "What happened?" asked William. "I took her to a party at Candice's friend's house. I was talking business with this woman and your daughter slammed a party hat onto my head in front of everybody!" "Why would she do something like that?" William asked. "I have no idea but I bet she won't do it again. I don't know what's gotten into her lately." "Dinner's ready!" Ronda yelled for the kids. Dinah and Joshua came running down the stairs eager to fuel their growing teen and preteen bodies but Annabella's door remained shut. "I'll go get her" said William. "Belly?" William said with a knock. "I'm here Daddy." "Don't you want to come eat?" he asked. "And why are you sitting in the dark?" he asked while flicking the light switch on. As he walked closer to the bed, there was a sudden change in his expression. "Oh my god! What the hell?" "Ronda! What did you do to her?" "Ronda came walking into the bedroom with a look that implied she had no idea what William was speaking of. "Look at all these welts on her!" William turned Annabella around consistently inspecting the marks. "They're everywhere! Why would you hit her like this?" "So it's okay for her to disrespect me?" she asked feeling victimized. "Put some clothes on baby." After Annabella was dressed, William picked her up and carried her out of the room toward the front door as Dinah and Joshua looked on in perplexity. "Where are you going?" Ronda screamed. "I'm taking her with me!" Breathing heavily, Ronda looked at Annabella with squinted eyes and clinched teeth. William grabbed Annabella's 'Teddy Ruxpin' from the couch before storming out with Annabella, slamming the door behind him. William sped off in his truck unsure of what to do or where to go. "It's okay baby girl. Does it hurt?" "A little but I'll be okay". Annabella didn't want to let on to her already frantic father of how much it hurt and how terrified her mother had made her. "Daddy, why did I have to stay at the Johnson's for so long?" Annabella asked. "For how long? I never knew you were there." Never mind Daddy. Just forget it." Annabella never found out why she was sent away. It didn't matter anyway. Annabella rolled the window down and stuck her head out. The cool air felt refreshing to her flushed cheeks and wounds and the lit-up sky helped to ease her weary spirit. That night, William and Annabella spent the night at a cousin's house. Annabella slept like a rock.

Ronda had made up her mind. She was not going to live in Olivia's house any longer than she had to. Unbeknownst to William, Ronda had purchased a new home located about forty-five minutes away from their current residence. William was furious but the new home was beautiful and it wasn't like they couldn't afford it. Besides, it seemed to make his wife happy and more comfortable and essentially, that's all he truly wanted. Things calmed down and even began to seem normal-for a little while.

One of Annabella's aunts on her mom's side of the family was having some financial troubles. Ronda sometimes tried to help her family when they were in need but her acts of kindness never seemed to come from a place of authenticity but rather from a necessity to feel needed or important. Vivian was the second to youngest of all Ronda's siblings. As a teenager, she was what many people in the South referred to as being "hot in the tail" or "fast". She was a fairly attractive woman and knew how to accentuate her femininity and sexiness. As a young woman, Vivian had slept with another woman's husband while she herself was married. Her husband left her after beating her to a bloody pulp and when word got around Grandburg, she was fired from the "Sack n Save" which was the only job she'd ever had. Vivian had a young son named Landon. He was one of the most adorable looking two-year olds one could imagine. However, he was also one of the most horribly behaved. He would bite, hit, scratch and generally injure people for absolutely no reason. He also refused to eat anything besides canned cocktail weenies and candy. Vivian couldn't control him and she even had to be pulled off of him after attempting to suffocate him with a pillow in the bed he shared with her. She would also give him long, cringeworthy kisses on the mouth that would make everyone uncomfortable. She was very odd. Vivian loved the attention men gave her. She was almost always scantily clad even when lounging around the house doing particularly nothing. One night, Annabella went downstairs for a snack and saw Vivian sitting on the stairs wearing a purple, short, silk robe. She was eating a bowl of grapes and offered Annabella one. "No thanks" said Annabella. As Annabella was walking back up, she noticed that Vivian was not wearing any underwear. When Vivian realized that Annabella had gotten a glimpse of her nether region, she tugged at the robe and turned to the opposite side of the stairway. Disgusted, seven-year-old Annabella went back up to her room to bed. Shortly thereafter, she heard her father come in late as he often did. Annabella wondered why her mother hardly ever waited up for him. Oftentimes, he'd come home and plop on the couch and if Dinah heard him, she'd come down and see if he wanted something to eat. Ronda would even tell Joshua and Annabella to go downstairs and scratch their father's back and rub his feet because she didn't want to. Ronda was never really the nurturing type. Immediately upon opening the door, William saw Vivian. He knew that she would likely try something. Ronda's family would warn the husbands and new boyfriends about Vivian. They were told to never be alone with her. She had hit on and slept with many of her sisters' boyfriends growing up and would often accuse them of either trying to seduce or even of violating her when it was not the case at all. While the warnings came off as simply being a joke, everyone in the family knew what she was capable of. Ronda knew it as well which further exhibited her need to do her best to keep an eye on her and William. William on the other hand, was not worried in the slightest. Vivian did nothing for him. In fact, he thought she was a repulsive slut. He did, however, think she had an incredible body and beautiful eyes. William admired the beauty in all women but there were some that even the testosterone filled, lady's man found no interest in. Besides, he was doing his best to continue to love and be a good man to Ronda despite the distance that had grown between them. “What are you still doing up?” he asked Vivian. “I was just eating some grapes and I thought I’d wait on ya since I couldn’t sleep.” “Well I’m about to go to sleep but thank you” William replied. He walked to the den and removed his suit jacket. He then sat on the couch and began to take off his shoes. Vivian walked over to the couch and bent down in an effort to help him undo his laces. “I got it” said William. He immediately stood up and went to the kitchen. Vivian followed him and began to try to rub his shoulders. “Vivian get off me. Don’t you know Ronda will kill you?” “I’m not scared of little ol’ Ronda” she said as she put her arms around his muscular abdomen. William grabbed her arms forcefully and shoved them away. “I’m going to bed.” He said. William walked up the stairs shaking his head. Ronda turned over in bed and woke up just enough to greet him. “Hey William. Are you just getting in?” “Yeah, I’m really tired. I’m gonna go take a shower.” William wondered if he should tell Ronda what had happened. Things were already rocky between them and he certainly didn’t want them to get any worse. He decided to keep the incident to himself and hoped that Vivian would do the same and that his rejection would thwart any further advances. Vivian had not yet gone back upstairs. She was angry and confused. She couldn’t believe he had refused her. She knew he didn’t love Ronda. She could see it in his eyes. “How could he love a woman so cold?” she thought. “They don’t even screw no mo from what she tells me” Vivian said to herself. The next day, things seemed odd around the house. Vivian was usually the loudest one but she was quiet as a church mouse. She scowled at Annabella as she walked by. Vivian used to be one of her favorite Aunts but there was something about her that Annabella no longer liked. Her aura was disconcerting. She even acted weird around Joshua but Annabella couldn't quite pinpoint what her problem was. That night, while getting ready for bed and after brushing her teeth, Annabella was walking down the hall. Vivian stuck her head out of one of the bathrooms and whispered for Annabella to come over to her. Reluctantly, Annabella walked back to where Vivian was. "Hey sweetie pie can you give this to your daddy for me?" Vivian handed her a letter written on wrinkled paper. "Don't read it though. Okay?" "I won't" said Annabella. Not being the sharpest knife in the drawer, Vivian neglected to put the note inside an envelope and all Annabella had to do was unfold it once to view its contents. Annabella was the best reader in her entire Elementary school. She actually read better than many adults. She knew she didn't have much time to read all of it before she got down the hall but during her quick skim, she was able to make out things like "You know it happened." "You just need to go on and tell her." Annabella may have been a young girl but she was far from stupid. She didn't believe it though. "Daddy would never do that." "She's so gross!" Annabella said to herself. Annabella knocked on the door. "Hey Belly!" William said. "You all ready for bed? Did you brush those teeth?" "Yep! Seeeeeeee?" Annabella said with a big, exaggerated smile. "That's my girl!" he said. "Daddy, Auntie Viv told me to give this to you." William's expression immediately changed. "Did you read it?" Annabella never liked to lie to anyone, especially her father but she couldn't tell him what she had read. After all, she knew it wasn't true. "No, I didn't read it." "What's it say?" Annabella asked. "Just go to bed baby." He gave her a quick kiss on the cheek and then shut the door. William read the note and immediately knew that he had to get that woman out of his house. He decided to show the letter to Ronda when she got home from the grocery store. When Ronda read the note, she went thru the roof! She chased Vivian around the house slashing at her with a filet knife. William was able to calm the situation down and thankfully, Ronda believed her husband. She knew Vivian's character and that was the last time she would try to help such an ungrateful two-bit whore. William paid for her train fare back to Grandburg and she was gone the very next day. Sadly though, this didn't help to strengthen the couple's union. In fact, after that, things went from bad to worse.

Thinking about moments of the past only aided in and fueled Annabella's yearning for the days when times were more loving and stable at home. It was Sunday night and William reluctantly brought Annabella back to Ronda's place. He hated having to drop her back off there especially because he knew what she went through every time she returned from one of their visitations. William knocked on the door with a sigh. "I don't think anyone's here" he said. "Me either". William went back to his truck and dialed Ronda's number from his truck phone. When there was no answer, William and Annabella drove away, much happier than they arrived. The next day was a school holiday so William took Annabella to work with him. She loved being in the office. Making coffee and Xeroxing documents always made her feel like a grown up. William had a lot of interesting clients. They all seemed to love and admire him not just for his work but also for the man that he was. He was very well-respected and likeable although Annabella knew that some of it was simply an act to get more business. Whatever he was doing worked and his success was not something to be ignored or denied.

The day was winding down and the sky began to show its telltale signs of amber calmness. It was one of Annabella's favorite times of the day and whenever she could, she would stand outside and take it all in. William came out to join her. "If only life could always be as beautiful as this" he said. Although William was born in Mississippi, he considered himself to be a proud Louisianan. After all, he had spent a lot of time there as a kid trying to escape the fury of 'Big Jo'. William had insisted upon having a tree of magnolia flowers planted in front of his business. Whenever Annabella would come to the office, he would always pick a flower and put it in her hair. "Dad, I don't want to go home" she said. "I don't want you to go either but you know you have to." "Go ahead inside and get your stuff. We'll go get something to eat and then I'll drop you off on my way to Laurie's." Annabella hoped that they'd get oysters on a half shell. She had only recently tried them for the first time and she thought they were delicious. William would always order two dozen of the shellfish and a nice tall, cold beer. Annabella would stare at him in disgust as he threw back the slimy looking creatures. Yet, Annabella was intrigued and began to think that if her father liked them, they couldn't be too bad. William showed her exactly how to make the dipping sauce. It consisted of hot sauce, ketchup, cocktail sauce, horseradish and fresh lemon juice. You had to make sure there was just the right amount of each to reach perfection. He would even give Annabella a few small sips of his beer because he always said that eating oysters with anything besides beer was nearly a sin against seafood. William teaching and exposing her to new things was one of the things Annabella liked most about spending time with her father.

Annabella dragged her feet into the back of the building to get her belongings. She wanted to call Ronda and tell her just how she felt-that she hated living with her and that she was much happier when she was with her father. Annabella had practiced for over a year what she'd say when the moment came but every time she thought she'd built up the confidence to announce her sentiments, nothing but air and silence would emerge from her mouth. Her mother never paid much attention to her and Dinah and Joshua never seemed to be around much at all. Annabella wanted a family-even if it wasn't the one she was used to.

Annabella heard some voices coming from the front of the building. She could make out that a woman was talking and she figured that William was talking to one of his clients that had stopped by. This was of course until she heard her name being screamed. "Hurry up Annabella!" Ronda had come to get her and she did not seem like she was in any mood to be kept waiting. "Wait, Ronda you can't just barge in here demanding things. I was going to bring her back in a few hours!" 'You were supposed to bring her back last night William!" "I tried but you weren't home." "You could've left her at Sandy's place and you know it!" "Look Ronda, I'm supposed to drop her off with *you!* I don't have time for these damn games!" he yelled. "Ohhhhh you don't have time? Is that because of all the sluts you have to free up your schedule for?" "That's none of your business Ronda!" "Annabella hurry up!" Ronda screamed. Annabella was packed but she didn't want to go outside. Ronda was angry and whenever she was heated, Annabella ended up being the one with the burns. "So, I hear you've got a new woman now." "I suppose you're gonna have some more kids too huh?" "I guess the three I gave you ain't enough!" "Don't you mean the *two* you gave me?" The silence that ensued was so grand, Annabella feared that they'd be able to hear her breathing way back inside the office. She covered her mouth and stood as still as a statue. "What the hell are you talking about?" Ronda's voice was no longer covered in a rough shrill. It now seemed more quiet, more calm. "Why don't you ask your sister what I'm talking about?" William replied glibly. "Yeah, Michelle was in town about six months ago". Michelle was Ronda's older sister. She and Ronda always had a bit of a sibling rivalry but they had also had their good moments. Michelle was a fairly successful woman. She worked for an automotive parts company and she made a very good living. Still, it always seemed as though Michelle resented Ronda. Michelle hated the fact that Ronda had moved away and married a successful man. Michelle accused Ronda of forgetting where she came from and insisted that she had been the only one to help out their mother and father when they were in need. Michelle had married Jasper Simms, an entrepreneur from Orlando, Florida. On the outside everything seemed fine but their home was not a happy one. Jasper had gotten hooked on cocaine and he began spending all their money on his habit. He had also started to become violent with Michelle when money was low and work was slow. Michelle had come to New Orleans on business and decided to stop in to see William. They always had a friendly relationship and she even figured that William may be able to help her or at least talk some sense into Jasper. In typical William fashion, he offered her a drink as they laughed and talked about old times and about her and Ronda's childhood. "What happened between you and Ronda?" asked Michelle pryingly. "I don't know Meesh. I loved that woman very much but things have honestly felt different ever since I got out of the Army." "I felt like I was giving so much but it was never enough. I just couldn't make her happy." "How about you and the kids? How's that going these days?" "Well, the baby doesn't hate me yet but those other two don't seem to care whether I live or die." William finished off his whiskey and cola and began to pour another- this time without the cola. Michelle slid her shoes off, stood up and then walked over to William, putting her glass out toward him for a refill. "Well, did you ever confront her about Todd?" "What about that motherfucker?" William's voice was now beginning to raise. He hated Todd. He always felt that Todd still wanted Ronda after she broke it off between them and deep down, William believed that if Todd wanted to, he could've gotten her back. He would have never dared to tell Ronda what he felt but it always bothered him inside. "Don't tell me you didn't know!" "I can't believe she would keep something like that from you!" "Spit it out woman!" William said, becoming agitated. "Bill, you've never wondered why Dinah looks different than Joshua and Annabella or why Todd's name was on the birth certificate instead of yours?" "My name is on Dinah's birth certificate." "Well, she must've had it fixed because when Ronda was recovering, Shirley was the one who filled out her paperwork and she told me that she put Todd's name in the space for the father." William's heart began to race. He started to think about all the times Ronda would hang up the phone the second he walked into the room and about Dinah's hazel eyes that he thought were so odd. "How could I be so stupid?" William wasn't stupid. He always felt like Dinah was Todd's but he didn't care. Ronda had even taken an entire bottle of Tylenol once Dinah's birth was near. She knew Dinah wasn't William's and she knew that everyone would know her secret. Thankfully, the doctors were able to save both her and the baby. William didn't let any of that stop him. He loved Ronda and Dinah and despite many warnings, even from his own blood family, he overlooked it all. However, Ronda had changed so much over the years. She wasn't the woman he initially thought she was. She was cold and her demeanor had begun to make him uneasy at times. "What's Shirley's number? I'm calling her right now." "Now what good is that gonna do ya Bill? You know that Shirley would never go against Ronda. They're the closest out of all of us." William put down the phone receiver slowly. Suddenly, he grabbed one of the many metal adornments on his desk and threw it across the room. It shattered the display case on his wall and glass went flying everywhere. Some of it landed in Michelle's hair. "I'm sorry Meesh" he said while stroking her hair trying to get the shards out." She grabbed his hand and they immediately became locked in a passionate embrace, kissing wildly, moaning loudly. Without any resistance, Michelle allowed William to throw her on top of his desk and rip off her panties and skirt. The more he thought of what he'd just heard, the rougher he became. That night, part of his soul was lost without a trace. Ronda had taken his heart and his pride and now, William had taken her sister. That was the last time he ever saw Michelle.

7

DIFFERENTLY ALIKE

Ronda didn't have much money growing up. While her father Vernon was a hard-working man, they were still unable to afford more than what they absolutely needed. They had to make do with what they had. Ronda would often tell stories about how she and her sisters would share the clothes that their mother Nettie had sewn for them. Nettie was a very fair-skinned African American woman. Pawpaw Vernon, on the other hand, was black as the night giving all except three of their offspring a darker brown hue to their skin. Ronda always felt as though Nettie showed favoritism to the ones that looked more like her. Ronda preferred the company of her father anyhow as she was what most would refer to as a tomboy. She loved skipping rocks in the lake, going on fishing trips and just about anything that involved getting dirty. Shirley, who was slightly older than Ronda, was very smart. However, she was often treated as being younger due to her frequent demonstrations of innocence. She loved to stay home with Nettie cooking and helping to take care of her younger siblings. Ronda couldn't stand all the domestic stuff and often avoided everyone altogether inside the treehouse that Vernon had built for her. Over the years, it had also become somewhat of a hiding spot for her when Nettie was not too happy with her behavior. One evening, Ronda was pressing her sister's hair straight with a hot comb so that she could go to a party. Ronda hated how she was always called upon to help her sister get ready only to be left at home with boredom and her bickering and often annoying siblings.

"Why don't you just use the wig this time?" Ronda asked Edith. "That thing stinks! It's already been worn to death as it is! Besides, Barry likes my real hair. He always says how pretty and shiny it is." "You know my hair is the most like Mama's" Edith said as she stroked the ends of her long, brown mane and stared into the cracked mirror she held in her hands. "If it's so much like Mama's then why I always gotta press it for ya?" Ronda said with a smirk. "Hush up stupid and finish me up! I'm gonna be late meetin' Barry!" Ronda was not very fond of Barry. She hated the way he stared at and winked at her while he chewed and smacked on his gum like a cow. He wasn't much of a gentleman and word had it that he'd been with nearly every girl in Grandburg. He was attractive though. Ronda just never cared for the frugal type. Edith always talked about how cheap he was and how he always made them share a burger and fries at the local diner. Sharing a shake was alright but a girl should be able to get her own burger and fries if she wanted. Ronda knew that any boy interested in her would have to have money and be willing to spend every dime of it on her if she so desired.

Ronda began to wrap the pressing comb in a towel to cool it off so she could put it away. "Why don't you press *your hair* first?" Grandma Nettie asked. "I'm fine Mama; maybe tomorrow." Ronda hated how her mother always made references to her hair not being good enough. Ronda never liked her hair and she often wondered if it were because of the things that her mother would say. Ronda wished she could flip and toss her hair and that it would flow effortlessly instead of simply being stiff and lifeless, like a helmet. Whenever she could get a hold of one, Ronda would stare at White women in magazines with their beautiful, luxuriously flowing locks. "One day, I'll be able to dress like and do my hair just like the women in the movies" Ronda thought. She swore she'd never be poor like her parents and that she would do whatever it took to get the things she wanted.

Ronda and her father were very close. Pawpaw Vernon considered her to be sort of like another son. He rarely saw her as a girl during her younger years. He even called her 'Ronnie' as a nickname due to her seemingly boyish ways. One day, when Ronda was about eleven years old, Vernon took her on a drive in his beat up red truck. He told her that he was taking her to go meet some family members that she had never seen before. When they arrived, there was a younger woman standing outside with two boys that must have been around thirteen and fourteen years old. Upon walking up to them, Vernon gave the woman a long embrace and a kiss on the cheek. The boys were well-mannered and handsome. They invited Ronda inside to go have some cookies and lemonade. "So you're my cousins or somethin'?" Ronda asked. They then traded awkward, indirect glances. The older boy took a quick sip of his beverage and with a shaky voice said, "We're your brothers." Ronda giggled, rolling her eyes at such a silly statement. "No you're not. I only have one brother and his name is Vernon Jr." "So is mine" said the older one of the teenagers. Ronda was dumbfounded. She ran back outside as quickly as she could. She found her father and the woman, sitting on the porch with her head on his shoulder. "Daddy are those boys your sons?" Vernon stood up like he had planned for the boys to tell her instead of him all along. "Yes, Ronnie, those are your brothers." "Does Mama know about this?" Vernon hung his head and stared at the ground. Ronda groaned loudly in shock and disgust and ran back to the truck and slammed herself inside. Vernon hugged the woman and came over to Ronda's window which hadn't rolled up for years. "You been runnin' 'round on Mama!" "Why?" "Ronnie..." "Don't call me Ronnie!" "I wanna know now Paw!" Ronda screamed. "Your Mama knows but I aint doin' it no mo! Me and Charlene care for one another but only as friends and parents to these boys." "I would never leave your mama!" "What about the others? Do they know?" No. and I don't want you tellin' em. You hear?" "Why tell me?" "Because I knew you could handle it and I at least want one of y'all to know about your other brothers." Ronda began to cry. She wondered why everyone always treated her like the strong one when she felt so weak inside. "I wanna go home" she said. Ronda never told anyone about that day and the bond between her and Vernon was slowly but surely beginning to crack and fall apart. Things were never the same.

Out of all the years her parents had been together, Annabella had never seen her parents kiss or even hug. She simply figured that the two of them were not big on public displays of affection and that perhaps they preferred to exhibit their love for one another in private. Annabella didn't understand this and insisted that when she grew up, she would shout the name of the man she loved from the highest mountain. She didn't care if anyone had a problem with it. Ronda seemed to equate love with material things rather than with people and emotions. She'd often brag about the trips William took her on and the amount of money he had spent on her shoes but Annabella never heard stories of actual demonstrations of what Annabella deemed to be true love and romance. After giving birth to Annabella, Ronda became very ill. Knowing that a member of the congregation was looking for work, William decided to call her up to see if she'd like to help take care of Ronda and the kids. He looked at it as friends helping out friends. The Garlands had known Ms. Francine for over a decade. Her being there was comparable to having another addition to the family. She would cook and clean, as well as keep Ronda company as she recuperated in bed. She'd make sure that Dinah and Joshua got to school on time and that baby Annabella was well taken care of. She stayed for about 3 months until Ronda fully recovered. She also babysat and sometimes helped out sporadically over the years when William and Ronda had business to attend to or vacations or outings to go on. One day, Ronda was talking to one of William's clients about housework. Four-year-old Annabella, was sitting on the floor playing a game when she overheard the conversation; "I just hate the smell of Comet" the client said. "I like the way it works but it just doesn't give me that clean smell I'm looking for." "My maid Francine uses bleach" Ronda replied. "It gives that germ-free smell." Annabella had never heard Ronda refer to Ms. Francine in that manner. Sure, she carried out some "maid-like" duties but she was their friend and hearing such a statement from Ronda was quite strange to Annabella. However, she figured that if her mother said it, it had to be true.

William and Ronda had put Annabella in a private school for part of her Kindergarten year. The students were adorned in deep red sweaters and plaid bottoms. They were allowed to choose their afternoon snack and lunch from a small menu handed out at the beginning of the day. The students spent most of their time painting or reading books that the ordinary Kindergartener would have likely found to be excruciatingly tough and/or boring. Annabella did not particularly care for the kids in her class. They were weird to her. She once saw a group of girls on the playground pricking their fingers with pins, rubbing them together and calling themselves "blood sisters". Annabella's parents had a thing about blood especially considering their religion forbade swapping or ingesting it in any form or fashion. This was even the case in terms of blood transfusions during even the most medically dire times and circumstances. The vampireesque children tried to get Annabella to join in but besides thinking it was utterly disgusting, she heeded her parents' warnings against such things. Annabella did however, temporarily fall in with the notion of material things giving more importance and meaning to one's existence. Being the only minority in her class and one of around five in the entire school, Annabella was often looked at as the odd one out. The other students and their parents were convinced that her being in their same learning environment had to be some sort of fluke and that she couldn't possibly be on the same level or doing as financially well as they were. Annabella grew tired of their snide implications and decided that the only way to alleviate the ridicule was to prove them wrong once and for all. Without asking for neither William nor Ronda's permission, Annabella invited a group of girls over to her home for a party. She told them about their two kitchens, two living rooms, colossal backyard and indoor "swim spa" as her parents so frequently referred to it. She gave them her phone number and told them to call for details. After about a couple of weeks without a mention of the festivities from her peers; Annabella forgot about the plans altogether. Apparently, one of the girls hadn't had the same lapse in memory. One evening, the girl's mother called to ask if the event would still be taking place. Ronda told her that she hadn't heard of any party and that she would speak sternly to Annabella about it as soon as possible. Overhearing one of the conversations, Annabella knew she was in big trouble. Ronda told William who laughed it off and even poked fun at his six-year-old daughter for even saying the term "swim spa". Ronda, however, felt the need to punish Annabella by either spanking her or taking away her favorite television show. Annabella absolutely adored the show "Pinwheel" on Nickelodeon and would rather have taken a beating any day than to ever miss an episode. Annabella thought it was unfair that her mother bragged all the time about their status and material items but expected something different from her children. Annabella later learned, however, that hypocrisy in her family would certainly never be tied to an isolated incident.

Ronda had recently gotten a job at a convenience store. Annabella loved going to work with her mother. Ronda would often let her price cans with a pricing gun and stock different items. Annabella hated being left home at only ten years old. She would often have to baby-sit CeeJay who was five years her junior. He was quite a handful but Annabella liked the company nonetheless. One afternoon, while both Sandy and Ronda were at work, Annabella was making a snack for CeeJay and herself. CeeJay was a rambunctious child and loved to jump around and play "Power Rangers" and "Ninja Turtles". During one of his escapades, he saw a large cockroach crawling across the floor. He went on a mission to kill it and grabbed a broken ironing board leg with a jagged edge. Annabella heard him scream, "It's in my skin!" and ran to his aid. The serrated part of the broken off piece of the metal had become lodged inside the skin of his hand. Annabella was horrified but was always taught never to call the ambulance or police when the two of them were illegally left home alone. Instead, Annabella called Ronda and Sandy at work. Ronda couldn't leave but Sandy rushed home and took CeeJay to the hospital. He ended up being fine but Annabella hoped that eventually, her mother and friend would come up with better childcare options.

Going to the convenience store with her mother wasn't a very safe alternative but at least she wasn't being left alone. Amnabella found the customers to be quite entertaining. There was one elderly lady in particular that Annabella especially got a kick out of. Everyone called her 'Crazy Agnes'. Judging by her appearance, the woman must have been in her '70s but her spunk certainly defied her age. She was clearly homeless and her hygiene displayed this factor tenfold. She would come into the store and poke the roasting hot dogs with her bare fingers only to claim that they weren't "done enough". Agnes did this on quite a regular basis causing Ronda to have to throw the hotdogs out, sanitize the machine and start all over. This of course cost money, not to mention aggravation. Eventually, Ronda reached her breaking point and told the woman to get out of the store and never come back. "Get out of here! Go on!" Ronda shouted. The vagabond- drunk, delirious and racist, began to shout slurs and knock things off the shelves. "Kiss my white ass, nigger!" replied Agnes while raising her skirt to reveal her pale, bare buttocks. Suddenly, the woman squatted and began to pee all over the store floor. Ronda, shocked and disgusted, instinctively grabbed a mop and began to shoo Crazy Agnes out of the door. Luckily, a local cop was coming in for his regular sixth cup of coffee. Fortunately, he was able to subdue and apprehend Crazy Agnes.

Things at the store weren't always so exciting and rambunctious. One day, while doing a crossword puzzle,

Annabella heard a voice over her shoulder say, "The answer's pumpernickel." She looked up to see a red-headed White man in a firefighter uniform standing behind her. Not being very fond of strangers, Annabella rolled her eyes slightly and looked back down at her puzzle. "Annabella don't be rude. This is my friend Kirkland" Ronda said softly. "Hi" Annabella replied timidly. "It's nice to meet you Annabella" Kirkland responded with his hand extended. Annabella shook it hesitantly. After a couple of weeks of Ronda dating Kirkland, Annabella got used to the idea of her mother having a boyfriend. The more time she spent with him, the less Ronda yelled at and beat on Annabella. Unfortunately, things didn't last and Ronda called off the relationship. She claimed that his parents were old bigots who didn't approve of their union. She also worried that because Kirkland was White, he'd kill her in some type of raging fit like she'd seen so many times on those cheesy TV movies. Ronda never tried dating outside of her ethnicity again. Kirkland was Ronda's first and last formal relationship after William and from then on, she merely used men for what they could give her. Annabella could always tell when her mother was going to go see a man or when she was prepping herself to ask a man for money or a favor. She would often take frequent and long bubble baths and overuse certain feminine hygiene products. The men would help out but Ronda never had anything to show for it. Annabella wanted her mother to be happy and even marry again but Annabella also knew that Ronda was struggling with some serious issues that needed to be addressed and remedied before she could ever be in a successful, loving relationship.

Annabella was now a preteen. She was growing into a very lovely young lady. She was not quite out of her awkward stage but the weight loss was beginning to give her more confidence in herself and her abilities. She had made many friends and although Ronda often allowed her to visit a few of their homes, none of them ever came to hers. Annabella figured that it was likely due to where they lived and although this hurt her feelings, she grew to understand the situation and she knew that the "ghetto" was not safe for anyone, especially children. However, Annabella began to grow tired of never having anything fun to do or anyone her own age to play with or talk to outside of school. Annabella's best friend Shanna was always busy during the summer so Annabella rarely got the chance to hang out at her house during that time. Annabella thought that Shanna had a great family life. She came from a good home. Shanna lived in a basic two-bedroom apartment when they met in the 5th grade but they eventually moved into a four-bedroom house. Annabella loved the relationship Shanna had with her parents but more than that, Annabella admired the marriage that Shanna's parents had. They seemed to love one another a great deal and for Annabella, especially considering what she was still going through, visiting their home was a breath of fresh air. One weekend, Annabella was allowed to sleep over at Shanna's. They watched horror movies and pigged out as they usually did when they were together. "It sucks you have to leave tomorrow" said Shanna. "I know, and you never have time for me anymore!" Annabella frowned funnily and softly swung a pillow at Shanna's head. "Why don't you try out for softball?" Shanna asked, as if a light bulb had just suddenly illuminated on top of her head. "No, I don't think we have the money" Annabella said sadly. "No, it's not that expensive. You just need a mitt, cleats and twenty bucks for two uniforms." "That's easy for you to say but I'll ask my mom." Annabella hoped that Ronda would let her try out. Ronda was never interested in anything that Annabella wanted to do. Factually, Ronda wasn't very interested in anything that didn't directly involve her. Annabella hated that their religion didn't encourage nor seem to allow involvement in any extracurricular activities considering how much Ronda liked to brag on her kids' so-called abilities. Luckily for Annabella, Ronda was not as involved in the regular activities of the church as she once was. The next day, when Ronda picked her up from Shanna's, Annabella was beyond nervous and hesitant. Ronda had her regular standoffish attitude but she at least smiled at Annabella for once in what seemed like an eternity. Now was her chance. "Mom, I was wondering if I could get involved in sports this summer." "You?" "In sports?" Ronda chuckled. Any time Annabella seemed too happy or excited about something, Ronda would accuse her of "acting White or weird". Annabella always hated the term "acting White". She had heard it enough at school from her African American counterparts whenever they wanted to attack the type of company she kept or the way she carried herself. Annabella had one or two Black friends but most of them were either White, Asian or Hispanic. This was not at all done on purpose. Some believed that Annabella may have thought she was better than the other Black children in her school because of the way she spoke or because of her differing taste in music but this couldn't have been further from the truth. She liked people who were nice to her and that was all there was to it.

"Well, yeah, Shanna plays softball and since I don't do much during the summer, I was hoping that I could maybe try out." Annabella closed her eyes tightly, waiting for the denial. "Well, I guess so." "How much is this going to cost?" "Shanna said I only need cleats, a mitt and twenty dollars for uniforms." "Only huh?" "If that's what you want to do

Annabella, I don't care." Annabella wasn't bothered by her mother's attitudinal response. She was simply thrilled that she was going to get to try out and do something different for once. Ronda took her to the sports store and got her what she needed. Annabella couldn't have been happier. However, Annabella wondered why her mother was being more pleasant than usual. She did however, roll her eyes each time Annabella seemed to let the excitement of her future athletic endeavor seep from within.

When they pulled up to their apartment, Ronda hopped out of the car and seemed to sail to the mailbox. Annabella, who was still gathering her things, watched from the car window as Ronda pulled out and sifted through the mail. Suddenly, Ronda began to dance and jump around almost toppling into the street. "Go inside. I'm going next door to Sandy's!" After putting her things away, Annabella also went over to Sandy's. CeeJay was playing video games. Annabella sat down to join him. "What are they talking about?" Annabella asked. "I think we're going to Six Flags" CeeJay replied. Annabella was happy but she hadn't been on a vacation that didn't at least involve her father since the divorce. She knew that it wouldn't be the same but she welcomed any chance at normalcy that she could get.

It was a Sunday afternoon and Annabella had been feeling queasy all day. Her head was pounding and her stomach ached terribly. She felt as though she needed to defecate so she went to the bathroom. All she could do was pee. After wiping herself, she looked at the toilet paper. It was covered in faint red blood. The toilet water was also partially red. Annabella knew she had started her period. She didn't know too much about her body because Ronda had not allowed her to take the sexual education course offered to the girls at school. Ronda also refused to have talks with Annabella about anything of the sort. Annabella took a shower and put on a sanitary napkin. Ronda came home in her usual mood. She was yet again, griping about losing an important document and she was frantically looking through boxes and old backpacks. "Mom, I think I got my period" exclaimed Annabella. "Well, go put on a pad!" yelled Ronda, giving Annabella a strange look that also seemed to imply a bit of disgust. "I already did" replied Annabella. "Well, what the hell do you want me to do? Come and look at the damn blood in your drawls?". "Never mind", said Annabella. Annabella hoped her mother would have been more sensitive to the subject but she was learning not to expect too much from Ronda when it came to sentimental occurrences. She simply wasn't "that type" of mother.

Softball tryouts went just as expected for Annabella. She wasn't very good at all. Most of the other girls had been playing for six years and this was Annabella's first crack at the sport. She hit the ball a few times and ran around the plates. The supervising coach wasn't impressed but yet, he put her on a team. It wasn't Shanna's team but Annabella didn't care. She was going to have a great summer! Ronda hardly ever came to see Annabella play. The two times she did come, Annabella wished she hadn't. She and Dinah sat in the stands and laughed at Annabella and her mother often teased her and said she "ran like a duck." Annabella hated their ridicule and it was actually quite embarrassing. Annabella began to think that maybe they were jealous. Both Ronda and Dinah had gained a substantial amount of weight over the years. Dinah had gone from what some called a "brick house" to a mini mansion and Ronda's stomach protruded far enough for some to mistake her for being with child. Annabella was physically fit and blossoming more each day. She felt healthy and was glad to be doing something active and worthwhile.

After several times asking, Joshua finally made some time to practice with Annabella. It had been a long time since she felt like she had a big brother or any type of familial structure at all. He taught her some tricks and how to hold her hands properly when throwing and catching. He worked with her on following through with her swings and not being afraid of the ball. He even taught her how to bunt. She actually got better and eventually was good enough to score a run for her team for the first time. Annabella's coach had taught her how to slide and as nervous as she was to try it, she followed his directions and went for it. The assistant coach was so proud of Annabella that she picked her up and swung her around a few times saying "You did it! You did it!" Annabella was so happy. The only thing that could have made that night better would have been to look up and see someone from her family cheering and shouting on her behalf. That same night, Annabella came home and called William. "Dad no one came to my game and I scored! Why weren't you there?" Annabella yelled. "You know I have to work Annabella and you need to watch who you're talking to like that!" Don't you ever raise your voice to me again!" Annabella slammed the phone down without saying another word. She ran downstairs to the living room and dove face first into a couch pillow, sobbing loudly. "No one cares about me or anything else anymore! I hate this damn family!"

During his split from Ronda, William would often take Annabella to Ms. Tabitha's and Mr. Jimmy's house. William had known Mr. Jimmy for decades. Jimmy was a friend of Big Jo's and often bore witness to the manner in which 'Big Jo' disciplined his children- mainly William. In fact, the reason why Jimmy and 'Big Jo' ended their friendship was because of the hot pepper incident. When Mr. Jimmy found out, he told 'Big Jo' that he had "gone too damn far". When things nearly came to blows, Jimmy knew that it was time to separate himself from his former buddy altogether. Mr. Jimmy moved from Mississippi to Louisiana in the '70s. When William returned from the Army, he and Mr. Jimmy got reacquainted and became very good friends. By then, Mr. Jimmy's first wife had passed away and he had married Ms. Tabitha. Annabella really liked Mr. Jimmy. He was a very kind, calm man. William used to make Annabella read the newspaper to him because his eyes had gone bad, plus William always loved showing off Annabella's incredible reading skills. Mr. Jimmy's wife Tabitha or 'Tabby' as William loved to call her was as sweet as sugar. She had thick bifocals and was so full of life and light that those who met her couldn't help but love her at first sight. She and Annabella played cards, watched game shows and Annabella loved telling Ms. Tabby new jokes. She smoked two packs of cigarettes a day and her cackle was hilarious and somehow soothing to Annabella. Annabella was never close to either of her grandmothers so being with Tabby seemed to fill a place in her heart that she always felt was missing. The only complaint that Annabella as well as many others had with Tabby was that she had a serious gossiping problem. This wasn't the type of problem that many women seemed to have. Tabby's case was severe. She gossiped to the point that it actually hurt those around her and caused many people to stop speaking to her completely. What Tabby didn't seem to realize or possibly not care about was that there was a big difference between talking about other peoples' business and telling a secret that a dear friend told her in strict confidence. Another thing that bothered

Annabella was the way Tabby spoke about her own daughter, Samantha. Samantha was very beautiful. She had long black hair, lovely eyes and gorgeous, creamy skin. Judging from her graduation picture, Annabella also assumed she was smart as well. “Ms. Tabby, when are you gonna invite Samantha over?” Annabella asked, holding the picture frame in her hands. “You don’t want to meet her crazy ass.” Annabella had heard of people be referred to as “crazy” but it was usually in a lighthearted manner. Certainly she didn’t mean that her daughter was crazy like those people Annabella sometimes saw in the streets holding Bibles and shouting at the sidewalk. Annabella asked about Samantha all the time but Tabby always gave her the same answer. Later, Annabella discovered that Samantha’s husband had died suddenly from a mysterious illness. He was the love of her life and Samantha’s fragile psyche couldn’t handle it. She was never the same after losing him. Annabella thought it was very mean of Ms. Tabby to refer to her daughter as “crazy” after what she had been through but in the South, especially among the Black community, it wasn’t uncommon for families to make light of or ignore mental illness altogether.

As usual, after driving home from picking Annabella up at school, Ronda went to the neighborhood mailbox. Annabella was waiting for her mother to come unlock their front door so they could go inside but instead, she heard laughter and hooting. Annabella figured that it had something to do with money because that’s the only time she ever saw Ronda seem happy. Ronda ran next door to Sandy’s apartment. Annabella followed. Ronda showed Sandy what had come in the mail. It was a settlement check from the divorce. Annabella never knew the amount yet it had to be decent for Ronda to be reacting that way. They began to laugh loudly and dance around. “So does this mean we can take these children on a trip?” Sandy asked hopefully. Ronda looked at Annabella and rolled her eyes. “I guess so girl” Ronda replied.

Annabella and CeeJay were so excited. Annabella wasn’t too pleased that they had to go to a religious convention on the way first, but she and CeeJay would take a vacation any way they could get it. Prior to the news of the trip to Houston, Ronda had told Annabella that they would finally move out of the bad neighborhood they were currently living in. She promised Annabella her own room with full-sized bunk beds. It’s a good thing Annabella didn’t hold her breath because it was apparent that Ronda had forgotten all about those promises. Annabella grew tired of hoping for something that would probably never happen. The settlement only further fueled Ronda’s desire to spend frivolously and continue to fight William in court. With that, in turn, came more lawyers’ fees. Annabella realized her mother enjoyed the drama of it all no matter what it was costing herself as well as her children. Nonetheless, the trip started out pretty good. Annabella was super thrilled to go to AstroWorld. She hadn’t been there since she was six. It was bittersweet though. Annabella wished that everyone were still together and that they could enjoy the fun as a family. She was however, glad to finally be doing something positive with her mother.

The Texas heat was brutal that summer. You could almost feel the moisture being sucked out of your skin. Annabella didn’t really mind the heat too much. She just didn’t like all the complaining Ronda was doing. Ronda never liked being in the sun too long. She was already ashamed of her dark skin and she certainly didn’t want it to get any darker. Ronda was always warning Annabella about staying outside too long. She would say things like "Yo ass betta come inside, you gon get Black!" Annabella in no way identified with what the big deal was. She didn't see why her getting darker skin was a problem. Ronda decided to stop at a nearby store to buy some sunscreen. They would be heading back home in two days so Annabella didn't see it making much of a difference. As soon as they got into the car, Ronda began to apply the lotion profusely. " I hope this stuff works well under makeup" Ronda exclaimed. "Here Anna, but some on!" "Um, no thanks" Annabella replied. "Girl, you better put this on!" "You gonna be black as a motherfucka if you don't." You already got like two shades darker already!" Annabella grabbed the bottle and slowly started rubbing the cream on her forearms. "Put it on your face!" yelled Ronda. Annabella began to rub in a circular motion on both cheeks only to feel a heightening, fiery burn. Annabella began to scream and cry, "It's burning; it's burning!" Ronda grabbed a bottle of water and handed it to Annabella. "Here girl, calm down, you alright?" Annabella poured the water on her face in hopes of alleviating the blaze. It helped but the damage had been done. For the rest of the trip, Annabella was in pain. Her skin was dry and scaly and wouldn't heal completely for weeks to come.

8

RECEPTION AND DECEPTION

Dinah was gaining more weight every day. She had begun to eat to the point that it disgusted Annabella. Dinah had found several of Ronda's old checkbooks. She would often order pizzas and Chinese food and pay for it with these checks, unbeknownst to Ronda. Sometimes, she would share but Annabella knew that too much junk food would only slow her down and she certainly didn't want to be less successful at softball than she already was. Dinah would often hide the takeout boxes under her bed. There were also times that she would put so much Ranch dressing on salads that Annabella wondered what the point was in eating salads at all. There was this one dish that Dinah absolutely loved. She would take condensed milk and pour it over white bread topped with sugared strawberries. She'd often wash this down with a root beer or Coca-Cola float. Annabella didn't know too much about fitness but she knew that the habits Dinah had developed were most certainly not healthy. Before the divorce, William had expressed concern over Dinah's weight gain. Many people had referred to her as being "stacked" or "fine" but William sensed that she was too endowed or "thick" for her age. Ronda painted him as an insensitive jerk for even commenting on such a thing but he insisted that he wanted his children to be healthy. Eventually, Ronda attempted to get Dinah to adhere to one of the famous diet programs that flourished in the '90s. This of course, was not before making sure to let Dinah know that her father thought she was fat and needed to go on a diet. Dinah always resented her father for that. Annabella wondered why Ronda felt the need to tell Dinah what her father had said to her in private. William never intended to hurt Dinah's feelings. Ronda could have simply cooked healthier meals for the family as a whole; that way, Dinah would not have felt targeted and singled out. Ronda loved making William look like the bad guy, even at the expense of her own children's feelings. William could be a bit insensate at times forgetting that some, if not most people, were more sensitive than himself. He did comment on Dinah's weight from time to time but he never used the word "fat". All William really wanted was for his daughter to be well and feel good about herself. Unfortunately, the meal programs Ronda chose for Dinah consisted of mostly snack foods and because Dinah mostly indulged in those along with continuing to still eat the other regular food in the house; she eventually quit the program completely.

One day after school, Annabella went upstairs to play video games. She saw Dinah rinsing her sheets in the bathtub. Annabella simply figured that Dinah had the flu or that she had eaten too much or maybe she had spilled something. Everyone in the family knew how clumsy she was. "You OK?" Annabella asked concernedly. "Not really" Dinah responded. "Sis, if I tell you something, do you promise not to tell anyone?" Dinah really trusted her sister. Although they were very distant in age, Dinah always felt that Annabella was mature and responsible enough to confide in. "What's going on?" Dinah looked up at the ceiling and let out a big breath of air. Then, Dinah slowly lifted up her shirt to reveal a big, pot belly. Annabella knew that Dinah was overweight but this belly looked different. Annabella pushed on it gently and it was as hard as a brick. "You're...pregnant?" Dinah was barley nineteen years old and Annabella knew that both Ronda and William would go through the roof if they found out. "Oh my goodness!" Annabella shouted, covering her mouth afterward. "Don't say anything. OK?" Dinah pleaded. "I promise. I won't tell" Annabella said, her hand still over her lips. Annabella kept her promise and she didn't tell a soul. The weight gain made more sense now but Annabella still believed that something deeper was at the root of it all.

Luckily, for Dinah's sake, she was able to hide her pregnancy from everyone until her eighth month. Dinah knew she had to come clean for her baby's as well as for her own safety. Ronda reacted surprisingly well. In fact, she wasn't upset at all. Annabella wondered how their mother would've reacted if it had been her instead of Dinah at that same age, in that same predicament. She probably would've thrown her out of the house but not without countless insults to go along with the eviction. William was upset about the news but after the divorce, Ronda constantly made him feel as if he didn't have much of a say-so in *her kids'* lives. After all, Dinah was legally an adult anyway.

Word got out regarding Dinah being with child and it wasn't long before the issue had to be taken up with the elders at the Kingdom Hall. Pregnant Dinah was taken into a room of males and asked sexual, personal questions. They threatened to shun her from the congregation if she didn't make an announcement of regret of her unborn child and her relationship with Craig. She refused to do so and hence, she was disfellowshipped. Ronda was upset about this decision but what absolutely made her seethe was when she assumed that William would also suffer the same fate after his non-marital escapades became public. William was a very well-respected elder. He had also donated a great deal of money to the organization. As with most forms of organized religion, sexism was alive and well. Therefore, no action was taken against William. Ronda, ignoring the humiliating ordeal her daughter had gone through, focused all her energy trying to get the elders to disfellowship her former husband. When her pleas fell upon deaf ears, she disassociated herself from the Jehovah's Witnesses. Annabella was happy to be free no matter how severely misplaced her mother's reasoning was.

A few months after their daughter Cassidy was born, Dinah and her childhood sweetheart, Craig were headed to the altar. Annabella really liked Craig. He was always very respectful and kind. Annabella gladly welcomed him into the family and was happy to have another big brother. Annabella was also very happy for her sister but Dinah was very young. Plus, the nuptials couldn't have come at a worse time. The day of the wedding happened to be the exact date and time as Annabella's final softball game of the season. Her team and Shanna's team were the last two standing and Annabella was super excited to play against her best friend. Instead, there she was, getting overly dolled up in a peach colored frou-frou dress and pompadour-like hair when all she wanted was her cleats, mitt and uniform. She loved Dinah more than any softball game so she sucked it up to be there for her big sister.

Dinah looked beautiful. Her lips were painted ruby red and her dress was pure, classic white. Annabella thought the choice of dress color was kinda funny considering the fact that baby Cassidy was in the wedding as well. The venue was very small being only enough room for an intimate wedding. Craig was dressed in a basic tuxedo and the bridesmaids wore chocolate brown dresses. William Jr. gave Dinah away. William Sr. and Dinah had an argument over the wages he was paying her while she worked at his office causing her to exclude and ultimately ban him from the wedding and any of the other matrimonial planning and festivities. The banquet consisted of hors d'oeuvres such as Swedish Meatballs and finger sandwiches. The ceremony went on without any issues. Prior to Cassidy coming into the picture, Ronda and Craig's mother, Edna were at each other's throats. Edna thought that Craig was too good for Dinah because he was in college and Dinah barely graduated high school. She and Dinah got along but she always felt that Craig could do better. She would also take jabs at Dinah's weight in the most passive-aggressive ways. Ronda never lost the mindset that the Garlands were once a prominent Black family and in her mind, Dinah was damn near the heir to a throne. Edna hated Ronda's stuck-up attitude and their disdain for one another certainly wasn't put on hold for the wedding of their children.

The ceremony portion of the wedding was over and everything seemed to be going fine despite a few dirty looks between the two mothers-in-law and them attempting to avoid each other altogether. Fifteen- year-old Joshua had been drinking with William Jr. before the ceremony began and it was definitely apparent in his behavior. At the reception, Joshua was flirting with every girl in the wedding party although most of them had boyfriends. One of the significant others was actually in attendance and he and Joshua had a few words during the reception. Both Joshua and William Jr. were not ones to be "punked" and decided to take their issues with the guy outside. Ronda tried to talk some sense into Joshua but he was already too riled up despite him being in the wrong regarding the entire situation. Ronda overheard Edna telling a friend that this was exactly why she didn't want her son marrying into such a family. This infuriated Ronda and while she was walking down a flight of steps, she purposefully threw a three-liter soda bottle down the stairs, causing the dark colored liquid to spew all over the wall and floor. Meanwhile, Joshua and William Jr. were still outside exchanging words with the bridesmaid's boyfriend. When they all decided to get into their respective vehicles; everyone watching from the upstairs window thought that all would be well. As they started to drive away from the premises, the boyfriend rolled down his window and shouted profanity laced insults at Joshua and William Jr. This was only met with William Jr. pulling out his gun and pointing it directly at the boyfriend through his truck window. The girls watching from the reception hall window gasped and one of them nearly fainted. Thankfully, nothing major happened and no one was hurt. It was a very interesting event to say the least.

A few days later, Ronda and Sandy were playing their weekly game of cards and having some beers. Annabella and CeeJay loved watching their mothers play cards, especially when they were inebriated. They started talking about some ongoing divorce court proceedings and Ronda began to laugh. "Girl, he really thinks he's got that judge fooled. I came in there and they saw little ol' me and thought he was a monster!" she laughed. Ronda often used her size to her advantage. After all, who are most people likely to side with?- a petite, demure woman or a mammoth-sized Black man with about as much arrogance as a peacock with the fullest of feathers? Ronda began to rub her eyes as she often did when they became dry because of her contact lenses.

"Ronda, why don't you just wear your glasses and take them uncomfortable things out sometimes?" Sandy asked. "Honey, you know I only take my contacts out for court!" They cackled loudly high-fiving each other from across the table. Ronda thought that her natural colored brown eyes made her look sadder, almost like a puppy dog. She could also cry right on cue and would gladly turn on the waterworks at what she felt were apropos moments. It was unclear whether putting on these facades came as advice from one of her many divorce attorneys or if they were things she had thought up all on her lonesome. Ronda changed lawyers like underwear. If one couldn't get her what she wanted at the exact moment she wanted it, she gladly traded him or her in for a new one. This ended up being quite costly for her but she knew that she'd clean up in the divorce. She felt like William owed her big time and she was hell bent on getting each and every penny she felt she deserved. Annabella had a habit of listening in on conversations. It could have been that she was a naturally curious child or maybe she was just plain nosey. She'd often wish she could have unheard certain things because they all too often remained with her long after they'd left and become distant memories to others. Upon one eavesdropping session at the bottom of the stairs, she overheard Ronda talking to her attorney in the living room on speakerphone. Ronda had insisted upon getting an office-type phone for their apartment. After all, to her, court had become a business in itself. "How much longer do I have to do this? This man has been living good while me and my children are stuck over here in this damn trifling ass apartment!" she screamed. "Ronda you know I'm going to do everything in my power to see you win but this is what it has to be for now. "Yeah, that's what the last two said" Ronda replied dismissively. "They were right and as your

Attorney, you'll just have to trust me. It'll pay off." Annabella didn't fully understand what the exchange was about but she always wondered why they lived in the ghetto when the child support alone would have covered the rent for a much nicer living space and neighborhood.

Joshua was beginning to become more defiant and unruly each day. Ronda worked late nights and was hardly ever there to supervise. He started to come home less frequently and sometimes not at all. Ronda never seemed to worry much while he was gone but when he returned she would often yell at and beat on him violently. Annabella would ask her mother why she didn't just call William and her reply would typically be, "This is my house, not your father's!" or "Mind your business Annabella!" One time, Joshua came in the door at around 2 a.m. and Ronda, who had the night off, was fuming. Once again, he had exhibited the reason why sixteen-year-olds are not meant to ingest alcohol especially not in large quantities. He reeked of regurgitated beer and cigarettes. He was clearly wasted and could barely comprehend anything at all but Ronda insisted on cross-examining him about the goings on of his night out. "Why is there throw-up all over your shirt Joshua?!!?" Ronda screamed. "Traaaaviiis" he replied sluggishly. "So, Travis threw up on the front *and* the back of your shirt?" asked Ronda tapping her foot in frustration. "Just leave me the fuck alone!" Joshua yelled plopping down into a nearby chair. This angered Ronda so much that she grabbed a leg that had broken off of an old coffee table and swung it with all her might striking Joshua's left knee. He screamed in agony and started to cry. Immediately realizing what she had done, she ran and got some frozen vegetables from the kitchen to apply to his injury. These types of exchanges became recurrent and all too commonplace in their home. It bothered Annabella in the beginning but after a while, she sadly started to become accustomed to the dysfunction.

Laurie had bought both Blake and Annabella expensive, handheld video game systems. Annabella was so happy that Laurie allowed her to take it back to Ronda's. She was often so bored with no cable television and without a decent and safe place to play outside, that she truly appreciated having something to do besides read the same books over and over or watch professional golf on the only television channel with a semi-clear picture. One afternoon after fixing herself a snack, Annabella thought she'd take another crack at beating her high score. She got a chair and placed it against the armoire in the living room. Annabella had put the game system up there because she didn't want anyone else to play with it and possibly break it. She couldn't wait to show Blake how well she'd done when her Dad picked her up for visitation Friday night. Annabella began feeling around with her right hand for the game but there was nothing there. "I know I put it up here" thought Annabella. "Maybe it fell." Annabella hopped off the chair and looked behind the armoire only to see pure darkness. She was confused. She had never placed it anyplace else yet she began looking in unlikely places like underneath the sofa, the bed; she even looked under the bathroom cabinet. It was gone. Annabella sat on the bed sobbing as Ronda walked in with a stack of documents. Annabella rolled her eyes in her mind. Annabella was so tired of her mother obsessing over the divorce and she wished she could just at least try to be a normal mom for once. "What's the matter with you?" Ronda asked uncaringly. "I can't find my Game Gear!" cried Annabella. "Oh, that stupid thing?" "You probably just misplaced it." " You know you're always losing things." Annabella cringed. She hated how Ronda attempted to act as if she knew her so well. Annabella was certainly not a forgetful child and she rarely lost anything. “Why would she care though?” thought Annabella. When Annabella first brought the game home, Ronda’s face was filled with jealousy and utter disgust. Annabella was so afraid for her to see the gift that Laurie had given her that she considered keeping it a secret from everyone. Then it hit her. “Maybe Mom threw it away!” Annabella’s stomach began to cramp. There was no way she could ask Ronda about it without feeling her wrath and she couldn’t tell her father because it would likely only incite another war between them. Annabella decided to keep on looking just to be sure. She tore the closet apart, looked under the seats of Ronda’s car; she even checked the kitchen pantry. Nothing. During her search, Joshua had come home. He was taking a shower and Annabella noticed that he’d left his bag on top of the couch, which he normally never did. Annabella remembered the time that Joshua had gotten caught stealing at the mall and it only aided in her belief that he could also have been responsible for her missing game. Annabella was scared because she didn’t want to get caught snooping around in his stuff. She knew he’d let her have it good if she did. Annabella lifted up the top flap of the backpack and felt around in the front pocket only to find some pens, pencils and the phone number of a girl named “Angel.” “No real angel would ever date Josh.” Annabella giggled to herself. Next, she opened the main compartment of the bag and found a pair of fake gold teeth, a hip-hop CD, a notebook and three little tubes full of tiny soap blocks. “It must be a new type of cologne or something.” “Boys are so weird.” Annabella whispered. Unfortunately, there was no Game Gear. Annabella cried the rest of night as she thought about what could have happened to it. She was devastated but what she didn’t realize was that she had just happened upon a discovery that would transform her family in the most damaging, irrevocable of ways.

Joshua had been hanging around a man named Randall lately. Randall was a new neighbor that had recently moved into the unit left of Sandy's. Annabella deemed their new-found friendship weird considering the fact that Randall was nearly fifty years of age. With Joshua being only sixteen, it was only right for Ronda to question and be cautious of such an unusual camaraderie. One night, after not coming home at the assigned curfew that Ronda had attempted to get Joshua to abide by, Ronda began to become worried. She called all of Joshua's usual knucklehead friends but none of them had seen nor heard from him in days, "Maybe he's over at Randall's place." Annabella suggested. "I told that damn boy to stay away from that old weirdo! Ronda yelled. "He doesn't listen to you anymore Mom." Ronda shot Annabella a glare that appeared to warn her to watch her mouth. "I'm going over there!" Ronda stormed across their poor excuse for a plaza and began banging on Randall's front door. "Open up! It's Ronda!" "Is my damn son in there?" Randall finally opened the door several screams and knocks later. He stuck his head out partially with his body placed strategically behind the door. "Can I help you?" Randall asked. "Is Joshua in there?" "No Ma'am; he's not" Randall replied. He attempted to close the door but Ronda swiftly wedged her foot inside. "You need to stop spending time with my damn son! Why the Hell does an old man with a Jheri curl want to hang out with a young boy?" "You'd better not be trying to molest my fuckin' son!" Ronda screamed. "Man ain't nobody ever gonna fuckin' molest me!" Joshua shouted suddenly from inside. Hearing her son's voice caused Ronda to lose all inhibition and push completely past Randall and go inside of his apartment. She rushed toward Joshua but not before glancing to the left of her at a table near the kitchen area. The table was covered with dozens of bags of marijuana and crack cocaine. The apartment also smelled like someone was burning chemicals. "Boy, don't you know that you're in a God damn drug house?" Ronda screamed. "I'm calling the police!" "Mom, come on. Don't do that!" Joshua begged. "Why?" Ronda asked. "Are you on drugs too?" Ronda began searching Joshua's pockets and looking closely and carefully into his eyes. "No Ma!" I'm not on nothin'!" Ronda frantically ran back to her apartment to call 9-1-1. Unfortunately, the police didn't usually show up when called in residences and businesses within bad neighborhoods. When they did, they'd often get there several hours after they'd been called. Randall had cleaned up and hidden all the drugs and paraphernalia by the time the authorities finally arrived. He also adamantly denied Ronda's accusations. Joshua refused to utter a word. Randall actually allowed them to search his apartment without a warrant. They found nothing. Randall moved out a few weeks later.

Not long after the incident, it had become quite apparent that Joshua was selling and perhaps even using drugs. He had stopped working with William due to them constantly butting heads. He sometimes didn't come home at all. His grades were suffering and he always had lots of cash even with being jobless. Ronda was ignoring all the signs and evidence of her son's recent endeavors. She and William were going through yet another court battle pertaining to their divorce. Whenever court and William were concerned, the focus that Ronda should've been placing upon her children, and even her own sanity, were engulfed in the flames of obsession that Ronda could never begin to extinguish.

9

CRYSTAL UNCLEAR

William had a home consultation to go on and he was not in a very good mood. He hoped the couple wouldn't be too difficult to deal with and that he'd be in and out of there as quickly as possible. Steven was an entrepreneur who lived on the Westbank of New Orleans in an old neighborhood. His family lived comfortably but they were currently having some financial issues. Steven invited William in. Their home needed a lot of work and as he looked around, William began to think that the job may have not been worth his time. The phone rang and Steven excused himself to the other room. "Can I get you something to drink?" he heard a woman's voice say. William looked up to be met by a fair-skinned woman wearing skin-hugging workout gear with an exposed abdomen. She walked to the refrigerator and pulled out a bottle of water. William tried not to stare but he was indeed impressed with her physique. Most of the women close to his age that he knew rarely took or had the time to exercise. He didn't find her face to be pretty, but long, straight flowing black hair seemed to make up for it a bit. "Got any Crown?" he asked. Do you really think it's the right time for that?" she replied. "When you want something, it's always the right time" he replied slyly. Crystal had a reputation. In fact, rumors seemed to imply that if secretions of the male anatomy had been bottled, it would have eagerly been her beverage of choice. William didn't seem to notice or care about the gossip surrounding his potential woman. William loved her voice. It was soft and subtle, something that he wasn't used to hearing especially having been married to Ronda for so many years. The chemistry between them was evident immediately and from the moment of their introduction, they had both forgotten that Steven was in the nearby room. Steven re-entered the area and stared at the two of them. He gave Crystal a glance and shook his head. He was so tired of her flirting with other men. It didn't seem to matter who the man was. If he had more money than Steven, he was on Crystal's radar. The fixing of the home had been her idea and Steven wondered if she had picked William personally, despite her insistence that he had been recommended by a friend of a friend.

William was definitely going to take the job now and he made it commonplace to show up only at times that Crystal had previously specified. After a while, Steven seemed to stop caring about his wife's wandering eye, amid her other body parts and he purposefully began to stay away from home more often each week. William and his new fling hardly had anything in common mentally but in the bedroom, they were completely in sync. She did things to him that no woman had ever done. She catered to his every need and gave him what he wanted whenever he wanted it. While Ronda was not a complete prude in the bedroom, she would turn her nose up at and reluctantly carry out oral sex although it's what William enjoyed the most. He actually enjoyed reciprocating it as well. He figured that a husband

and wife or a couple should have no limits in the bedroom and in that regard, Crystal was definitely a breath of fresh air. She had three children total-two girls with Steven and one son from a previous relationship. They were adults and teenagers which allowed her to spend a lot of time away from home going on rendezvouses with William. Things had gotten to be pretty serious between the two of them but because she was still married and had not yet brought up indications of a divorce, William still viewed himself a single man and continued to date other women.

One Saturday night, during one of his visitations with Annabella, William decided to introduce her and Crystal. William Jr. and his wife Klaudette had invited them over for a small cookout at their new house. They had just had a new baby and she was adorable. Annabella loved Klaudette. Annabella thought she and William Jr. made the perfect couple and that they really complimented one another. William Jr. had inherited some of the male side of the family's anger issues and Klaudette seemed to be the one person that could bring him back down to Earth when his temper overflowed and began to get out of hand. After picking Annabella up, they stopped at a local grocery store to pick up some wine and beer and the paprika that Klaudette had forgotten to pick up on her way home. Crystal had agreed to meet them at the store. Unbeknownst to them both, Annabella and her father's new woman had crossed paths when William was selecting the spirits after sending Annabella to the spice aisle. Annabella found her dad and they walked toward the registers. Crystal was already standing there with a bottle of wine in her hand. He walked over and kissed her on the cheek. "Belly, this is Crystal." "Hello, nice to meet you." Annabella said as they shook hands. Annabella could usually get a feel for someone right upon meeting them and the feeling she got wasn't a good one. She couldn't quite put her finger on it but she had this feeling of uneasiness the instant they touched hands. She had never felt that way about any of the other women her father had introduced her to. In fact, she really liked all of them. They arrived at William Jr.'s house and Annabella immediately ran to the room with Klaudette to go see the baby. William Jr., Crystal and William Sr. began fixing themselves drinks and had already sparked up a conversation. After getting the baby to fall asleep, they all went outside and started eating. Crystal didn't say much and while perhaps unintentionally, she came off as being a bit rude. Annabella gave her the benefit of the doubt and decided to chalk it up to her being shy being that it was the first time that she had met the family. They went back inside after a few hours for some more drinks. It was getting kind of late and William was beginning to nod off in the living room reclining chair. Annabella and Crystal were sitting on separate ends of a moderately long sofa with William Jr. between them. William Jr., being the jokester and instigator that he'd always been, turned to Annabella and asked, "So where did y'all stay last night?" Annabella had never been a very good liar and why should she lie? After all, her father was a single man. "We stayed at Ms. Laurie's house." Crystal gave Annabella a look that could uproot trees. She quickly grabbed her purse and stormed out of the door. Hearing it slam awoke William and he began to look around wondering what all the commotion was about. He realized that Crystal had gone outside. He ran out after her and caught her just before she could speed off. "What's wrong?" he asked. "So you wanna sleep at that bitch Laurie's house? Yeah, your daughter told me! Did you have fun?" "She's just a kid. She probably just got confused. You know I don't stay over there no more" he said pleadingly. Crystal rolled her eyes with a tear streaming down her cheek. She then sped off almost taking William's arms that were inside the window with her. William came back inside and told Annabella that it was time to go. Annabella was a little scared that William might be upset with her but Annabella did not feel badly at all and secretly hoped they would break up. The last thing Annabella wanted was to have another woman trying to come between her and her father. William and Annabella got into the truck and William pulled into the parking lot of a convenience store. Annabella assumed he was stopping in to grab a beer. Instead, they pulled up to a pay telephone. "Now why would you tell her something like that?" William asked. "Are you gonna whoop me?" Annabella asked nervously. "Hell no! I would never hit you over no woman!" Annabella knew the answer to that question before she asked it. It was just refreshing to here him say it especially because he had been spending so much time with Crystal as of late. "Can you just call her and tell her you made a mistake?" William knew that Annabella was much too intelligent to have made such an error but since Crystal didn't know her, he felt and hoped that it might be slightly believable. "But Dad, I don't want to!" "Come on, do this for ya daddy sweetie." Annabella loved her dad and hated seeing him upset. She figured that if he liked her, she couldn't be that bad so she went ahead and made the call. "Hello, Ms. Crystal?" "Yes" she replied smugly. "This is Annabella." "Hi Annabella." "Well, you know what I said at my brother's house? Well, I didn't mean to say that. I meant to say we stayed at Ms. Tabby's house. I just got a little confused." "Did your father tell you to call me?" "Well yeah but I wanted to do it anyway." Crystal didn't believe Annabella for a second but she thought it was a cute gesture. She wasn't ready to let William go. She was having fun and besides, she seemed to have him right where she wanted him. William took the phone from Annabella and he and Crystal began to talk. Annabella got back into the truck and watched her father through the windshield glass. When she saw him laugh she figured that the call had gone over smoothly. After hanging up, he went and got that beer along with some candy for Annabella.

William and Crystal were seeing a lot more of each other but William had still not completely cut things off with Laurie. Annabella wished her father would make better choices. Laurie would have made a great wife. William had finally convinced all three kids to come over for a get-together. He had invited some friends and family to a poolside BBQ. Cassidy was with Craig at his mother's house. Annabella was so excited. She loved having her family together. William had even invited Ronda but she had to work. Besides, when she found out that Crystal was going to be there, she nearly vomited at the thought. Annabella was relieved. She didn't want to endure the drama that would surely have ensued if her mother were around Crystal. William always took the opportunity at every cookout to make his famous 'Grilliam's Shish Kabobs'. Annabella loved staying in the pool until she was wrinkly as a prune. Dinah and Joshua felt they had gotten "too old" for swimming pool silliness and they preferred to spend their time conversing with the people their cousins had invited to the event. William was very protective of Annabella. He kept his eye on her the entire time she was in the pool. The party had begun to die down. William, as usual, had indulged a bit too much so he decided to let Crystal drive. Ronda's place was across the river so the trip would take about thirty minutes one way.

Once they arrived, Dinah waddle-ran inside because she had to use the bathroom. Annabella followed behind her. Joshua started talking to some guy that was standing inside the plaza. Annabella was happy that Ronda hadn't returned yet. She didn't want to go through the questions, dirty looks and the film of negative energy Ronda reveled in covering her daughter with upon her return from visiting her father. Annabella looked in the refrigerator. "As always, nothing good to drink" she said with an eye roll. She heard a bit of noise outside but she couldn't make out what it was. She figured Joshua should've been inside by this time so she decided to go outside to check on him. Shockingly, as she pulled the door open and looked outside, she saw Joshua fighting one guy and William pummeling another. Annabella ran upstairs to get Dinah. "Dinah!" "Josh and Daddy are fighting!" "Each other?" Dinah yelled. "No!" Some guys!" Dinah pulled her pants up and the sisters went flying back down the stairs. By the time they reached their brother and father, the guy Joshua was fighting ran across the street leaving Joshua bleeding from the nose. William was banging a different guy's head onto the concrete. Annabella saw the fleeing male enter an apartment. Almost immediately, about six guys, came out of that residence. William knew there'd be serious trouble. He got off of the guy he was beating and directed his children to head to the car quickly. Crystal was still inside in the driver's seat. The guys ran towards the Garlands. One of the guys had a gun and pointed it right at Annabella. He pulled the trigger just as William threw Annabella into the car. She never heard a gunshot because his gun had jammed. Normally, William would've had his guns but he had left them in his truck and opted to take Crystal's car instead. Luckily, her only redeeming quality was to flee from a dangerous situation effectively. She drove all the way back to William's apartment. William knew that he had to go back. If Ronda insisted on his children living in a neighborhood like that, he had to make sure it was safe for them. Despite the bad man that Ronda wanted everyone to believe William was, he loved his children very much and he'd do anything to protect them. Annabella was hysterical and begged her dad not to go back there. She knew her father was heroic and strong but he was outnumbered. Besides, he was still human. She didn't know if she could go on without her father. Dinah and Joshua were becoming more distant by the minute and Ronda hated her. Despite her pleas, her father had to do what he felt was best. He asked Joshua if he wanted to come because the whole ordeal had started with the conversation in the plaza. Joshua was understandably terrified and declined. Annabella refused to lie down let alone sleep until she knew her father was safe. Everyone else, seemed eerily calm. In fact, they were dozing off. Approximately three hours later, William entered the studio apartment. His white t-shirt was covered in blood and he had two black eyes on one eye and three on the other. He was also bleeding from his mouth. Annabella pretended to be asleep because he told her that she better not be awake when he got back. She heard him tell Crystal that he had killed one of the guys. Annabella didn't know if it were true until Sandy later told her that she saw him do so. After the incident, the neighborhood was safer than ever for the Garland children. Nobody ever bothered them. Still, Annabella hated it there and she longed to move somewhere where nothing like that would've ever happened in the first place.

During a visitation weekend, Annabella overheard a phone conversation between Crystal's husband and William. They seemed to be fighting over her and whose "property" she truly was. Annabella found this to be quite silly and wondered why her dad didn't simply back off and let Crystal be with and work things out with her husband. "Adults make things so difficult" she thought to herself. William yelled a few vulgarities and slammed the receiver down. Annabella was going to check on him but she thought he probably needed a little space. Secretly, she hoped that the husband had been the winner of their exchange and that her father would go back to his old self. Although he and Annabella were still close, she did sense a change in her dad. He seemed to be depressed and sometimes, even on edge. One night after picking Annabella up, she and William went back to his apartment. Crystal was standing at the window with her back towards them. When she didn't turn around when they walked in, Annabella figured something was wrong and that maybe they had gotten into an argument or something. "Hi Ms. Crystal" Annabella said. When she turned around, Annabella noticed that her right eye was swollen and extremely bloodshot. "What happened to your eye?" Annabella asked. "Ask your father" she replied. Annabella turned toward William and before she could ask him anything, he said "Oh, I threw something at her but I didn't mean to hit her with it." Annabella felt like there was more to it but she didn't want to believe that her father would ever harm a woman in the physical sense. After all, Ronda had made it blatantly clear and had even bragged on many occasions about the fact that William had never put his hands on her. "Why don't you just say you're sorry and buy her a gift or something?" Annabella asked. William didn't reply. Annabella went to a vending machine on another floor of the building to get a snack and give them a little time to talk. She had never seen her father like this before. This made her even less fond of Crystal but if William had indeed hit her, Annabella would never take her father's side on such a thing. Wrong was just wrong. They managed to get over whatever issues they were having but Annabella was still not convinced they were a good fit for one another. Usually, her father moved very quickly when it came to marriage which was evident in his relationships with both his first wife as well as Ronda but with Crystal, things seemed to be going at a much slower pace. Perhaps it was because she was currently married to someone else but she had finally separated from her husband and there were no laws against getting engaged to one man while being married to another. Annabella did not want her father to marry Crystal but she really didn't believe people should live together and not at least be thinking about making it official.

It was Saturday morning and William had to run to the office. Annabella and Crystal were still at the apartment. Annabella was asleep on the couch. She felt something touch her nose. She awoke to Crystal kneeling down in front of her smiling. "Come sit on the bed with me!" she said gleefully. This was the first time that Crystal had initiated a conversation with Annabella without William being around to encourage it. Groggily and reluctantly, Annabella walked over to the bed and sat as far away from Crystal as she could without making her discomfort very obvious. "Are you hungry?" Crystal asked. "A little." "Me too" Crystal replied. "You know what I could go for?" "A cheeseburger with strawberry preserves" Crystal said with a grin. "You mean like a sausage biscuit with preserves?" Annabella asked with a confused look. "No, I mean a cheeseburger from McDonald's" said Crystal. "That's disgusting!" "That sounds like something a pregnant lady would eat." Crystal began to blush with a huge smile on her face. "You're not pregnant, are you?" Crystal chuckled and nodded. Annabella's heart dropped. *She* was the baby of the family. She was already sharing her father with his new girlfriend. A baby would only make things worse. Annabella smirked awkwardly. "Okay." "Why didn't my dad tell me though?" "He thought it would be better for me to tell you." "Oh. Well.... congratulations." Annabella went into the bathroom and sobbed into a towel. She hoped she and her dad would still be close once the baby came. She wasn't going to let a baby break their bond though. They were best friends. Annabella collected herself and went back to the room. Despite her fabricated acceptance of the news, she didn't say another word to Crystal that day.

There was a bit of levity surrounding the situation though. Annabella knew her mother hadn't heard the news yet. Annabella knew how Ronda would react. She would act like Crystal was simply lying to "trap" William, or if Crystal was indeed with child, Ronda would deny that William was the father. Annabella did not necessarily want to hurt her mother with the news. But why should she be hurt? William had been with several women since the divorce. Besides, Ronda seemed to hate William with every fiber of her being. At times, the very sight of him nearly sent Ronda's blood pressure to the boiling point. Annabella was simply curious as to the manner in which Ronda would go about victimizing herself as she always did by way of her strikingly apparent delusions of grandeur and paranoia. It had been about three years since the split and Ronda still constantly talked about William. She would accuse him of tapping her phone and having her followed. If she met a man named William or anything similar, she would assume that William had sent him to her to retrieve information and report back to him. She would hoard legal documents on cases that had already been settled and she'd even keep his used napkins from times she managed to play nice enough for him to invite her to lunch. There were several times that Ronda and

William got along well. Once in awhile, William would let Ronda know that business might have been a little slow and that he'd appreciate if he could make partial payments of the child support once in awhile and pay the rest a bit later. She would agree to this only to turn around and demand it instantly when he wasn't behaving the way she wanted him to. If she saw a woman coming out of his building, she'd assume and insist that William must be in a romantic, sexual relationship with her. If Ronda did not get her way, it sent her into a rage and nothing else mattered besides getting her revenge. She neglected her children, her looks and even her own mental state because of her obsession with William's life. A once very beautiful woman had almost completely let herself go over a man she wished death upon and claimed to loathe utterly.

Annabella walked into the front door of Ronda's apartment ready for the routine interrogation from her mother. Ronda never kissed nor hugged Annabella when she'd return from her weekend visits with her father. Although this hurt Annabella's feelings, she had grown used to it. In actuality though, Annabella had no desire to receive nor reciprocate any affection with her mother. It was clear that their relationship would never be one that was based upon love. They simply had to tolerate one another until Annabella was old enough to live on her own. Annabella had decided a long time ago that she wouldn't reside under the same roof with her mother longer than she absolutely had to. The faster she could get away from Ronda, the better.

"So what did you and your *perfect father* do this weekend?" Ronda asked with a scrunched nose and sarcastic tone. "Not much. He had to work a lot" Annabella replied. "So what bitch did he leave you with this time?" Ronda asked, shuffling through a heap of papers. "I went to work with him on Saturday and I spent part of today with Ms. Crystal." "Hmmph!" "That bitch is so dumb, I'm surprised she could even communicate with you!" Ronda chuckled. Annabella smiled a bit inside. "Well Mom, Ms. Crystal *did* share something with me. She was hoping it would bring us closer together" Annabella said with a slight smirk. "Yeah right!" "That bitch will never be close with MY child!" "What did she share with you?" "How to be a whore?" Ronda laughed wickedly. "No." "As a matter of fact, she shared with me that I'm gonna have a new baby brother or sister." Ronda's face nearly turned inside out. It was almost as if she were malfunctioning. "Ha!" "That bitch ain't been no more pregnant than the man in the moon!" "I think she *is* Mom." "She's already having cravings." "OK, suurrrre." "That whore ain't pregnant and if she is, it damn sure ain't your Daddy's baby." "It'll probably die anyway. Her old twat can't carry a child." Annabella wasn't naive nor was she typically childish. She just wished her mom thought of her as a child and treated her with enough love and respect to not speak that way in front of her. It made Annabella very uncomfortable. No one besides William seemed to ever think of nor treat Annabella as the kid she was. Most of the time, she felt as if she'd been an adult since birth. Annabella attributed a lot of that to the religion she had been raised in. No holidays were allowed and they made sure that children knew as early as possible that anything full of wonderment, and magic besides Jehovah was off limits and wholeheartedly false and demonic.

William was beginning to drink more heavily and quite frequently. He had taken Annabella to a cookout at one of his cousin's houses. They were outside listening to music and drinking cocktails. William had consumed about seven of his signature Crown Royal and colas and was very drunk.

He had even called Ronda and told her that he was never going to bring Annabella home and that he wanted her to live with him. While this made Annabella very happy, she knew that things weren't that simple and that Ronda would fight for her despite not wanting her at all. She would never let William win at anything without a fight. Annabella was young but she knew that her father was too drunk to drive. It was Sunday though and he had to have her back to Ronda's so that she could go to school in the morning. It was a pretty foggy night and Annabella worried that her dad's inebriated state coupled with the bad weather conditions would surely be a disastrous recipe. Once they were in the truck, William's cousin Karyn came to William's window, handed him another drink, this time in a secured fast-food cup and said, "How about one for the road cuz?" Annabella didn't understand how people, especially adults, could be so irresponsible. She hoped William would turn it down or at least not drink it with her in the car but to her dismay, he grabbed it, took a long sip from the straw, kissed his cousin on the cheek and drove off. Annabella always had a lousy sense of direction but after a few minutes she realized that William had passed up the route to Ronda's place. She further realized his mishap when he swerved onto the toll overpass in order to cross the bridge to get to New Orleans knowing that Annabella lived on the Westbank. Annabella figured he was either doing this on purpose due to the conversation he had with Ronda in his stupor or because he forgot what he was supposed to be doing and was simply following their normal routine of going straight to Laurie's after he picked her up from Ronda's every other Friday. Annabella would've liked nothing better than to go along with whatever plans her father had but within, she was frightened and didn't want to be in the truck with William in this state for one more second. "Dad, this isn't the right way. You're supposed to bring me home tonight." "Remember?" "Oh. That's right!" By then, he was already in line for the toll so he had to keep going forward. Once he got to the booth he asked the attendant, "How do I turn around from right here?" She gave him a bit of a strange look and then guided him to go forward, make a left and then simply turn around. Annabella got home safely but she was very angry with William and also very hurt that he would put her life in danger like that. They pulled into the parking lot of Ronda's place and Annabella partially hopped out before he could turn the motor off. "What's the ruuussshh?" he slurred. "Dad, I don't like it when you drink and drive." "Listen, I'm the parent! You donnn't tell meeee what tuh do!" he yelled sloppily. "Well, if you do it again, I'm not going to come with you anymore!" "Get the hell out of my truck then!" William yelled, his breath coated in alcoholic fumes. Annabella jumped out of the truck with tears streaming down her face.

When she walked inside, Ronda was standing there with her proverbial, imaginary detective badge on ready to dive right in. "What's wrong with you?" Annabella didn't want to get her father into trouble so she responded with, "I don't want to talk about it." Ronda of course was not satisfied with that response and continued to pester her daughter. "You betta answer me girl!" Ronda said, raising her voice. "Dad is just being really mean right now and he made me upset" Annabella reluctantly replied. "Well, I told you that you'd see his true colors one day." "Mom can I just go to bed?" "I have to go to school in the morning and it's late." "Alright fine, but I don't know why you're acting so surprised." Annabella changed into her pajamas and closed her eyes really tight wishing she could be somewhere new and somebody else. At least she had her dreams. No one could take those away.

Fortunately, Annabella and William managed to work through the incident. She also finally got to spend some quality time with him which she thought wouldn't be feasible after the announcement of Crystal's pregnancy and with him working so much. Annabella had not adjusted to the baby news quite yet although the birth was only four months away. She had also found out that it would be a girl which only further worried her. She hoped she wouldn't be replaced as 'Daddy's little girl'. Perhaps William was beginning to sense Annabella's anxiety and thoughts because he took her out for one of the most fun times the two had ever shared. They went to their favorite Chinese restaurant. Annabella refused to leave until she mastered the chopsticks. She had seen William use them so many times and she could never figure them out until that day. Next, they went to the arcade in the Riverwalk where William won her every big stuffed animal imaginable playing basketball. The manager actually came out and asked William and Annabella to leave because they weren't leaving any prizes for the other customers. They both got a kick out of that and laughed and joked about it on their way back to Ronda's. Before Annabella got out of the truck, William handed her a small box. "I know you've been feeling a little down lately but Daddy loves you and if there's one thing I'm sure of, it's your love for me." This had become their special saying over the years. Annabella opened the box to see a gold tortoise pendant with an amethyst shell. Annabella had developed a love for tortoises on one of her and William's many trips to the Audubon Zoo. She was fascinated with how long they lived and that they could hide within themselves if they ever felt frightened. Annabella often wished she had this ability, and she never felt this more than when her visits with her dad came to an end. Ronda never seemed to like seeing Annabella's joy especially when it was related to William. Upon entering the apartment with her many stuffed toys in tow, Ronda was standing there tapping her foot. "He's always dropping you off late knowing you have school in the morning!" "We're only 20 minutes late though" Annabella replied. "In 20 minutes you could have taken a shower and already be in the bed!" "What's all that shit?" Ronda asked glaring at the giant plastic bag Annabella was carrying. "Daddy won these for me at the arcade." Why is he always taking you to that damn Riverwalk?" Ronda asked rolling her eyes. "We love it there. We *all* used to love it. Remember?" Annabella asked. "Go get ready for bed!" Ronda barked. Annabella decided not to show her mother the tortoise pendant. She knew Ronda would find a way to attempt to ruin that too. Annabella was in a great mood and she refused to let Ronda take it away from her. Not this time.

William and Crystal named the new baby, Alice. William always liked names that began with the letter 'A'. Dinah was the only exception to this trend that had begun with his first-born daughter. Alice looked just like William. Of course, Ronda saw no resemblance whatsoever. As she grew older she only looked more like him which sunk Ronda even deeper into the sea of denial. She insulted Alice every chance she got. Alice struggled a bit in her early years. Ronda would make jokes and imply that Alice was mentally challenged. She also continued to wish death upon the child. When Alice turned six, she had gotten very ill and had to have extensive surgery. Ronda specifically requested a court date for the same day as the surgery and petitioned that William have a warrant put out for his arrest for being a "no show" to court. William refused to *ask* the Judge or anyone else for permission to attend his daughter's procedure and simply did not go. This exasperated Ronda. She detested when she was not the center of attention-no matter what the situation may have been. After leaving the courthouse, Ronda drank boxed red wine (that she claimed to be so allergic to) and danced like she had never danced before. When Annabella called William to see how everything had gone, he let her know that her little sister had pulled through like a champ and was expected to have an excellent recovery. Simply seeing Annabella smiling on the phone seemed to drain every ounce of joy from Ronda's spirit. In her bathrobe, Ronda walked solemnly up the stairs, went into her bedroom and closed the door behind her. Annabella didn't see her mother for two days.

Dinah and Joshua never understood why Annabella didn't like Crystal. They thought she was really nice. They always thought she was pretty. One day, they were all sitting in the living room and Annabella asked them who they thought was prettier between their mother and Crystal. "I think mom is prettier!" shouted Annabella before her siblings could answer. Dinah and Joshua both gave each other a look and a smile that immediately broke into an air of laughter. "What?" asked Annabella. "You're only saying that because you don't like Crystal and because you're scared of Mama" teased Joshua. It was true that Annabella was fearful of Ronda but this never stopped her from having her own opinion on a subject-especially such a trivial one. "You guys think Crystal is prettier?" "Eww!" "Why?" Annabella frowned in disgust. "Her hair is way prettier and longer." "Plus, she's light skinned" replied Joshua. Dinah sneered and then looked down when Annabella gave her a glance of disapproval. "I think Mom is way prettier. She has beautiful smooth skin, a cute nose and pretty brown eyes when she's not wearing those dumb contacts." "Crystal has wrinkles already, her nose is too big, and she's hairy and never shaves her armpits or legs!" "Ick!" yelled Annabella. "Yeah, but mom's fat!" said Joshua. Dinah's smirk dissipated immediately as she excused herself from the conversation to go to the restroom. "Yeah, but Mama can always lose weight!" said Annabella. "Besides, I asked Daddy and he said Mom is prettier too!" yelled Annabella. "He just lied to make you feel better" Joshua said with a laugh. "Whatever." Annabella replied with a head shake. Annabella wanted to tell Ronda what her two favorite children had said about her but she probably would not have been believed anyway. Annabella thought to herself, "It doesn't matter what I think. She doesn't even like me anyway." Despite this realization, Annabella would have never put another woman above her mother. Their tumultuous relationship did not mean that she didn't love Ronda but it was getting more and more difficult to attempt to like her. Annabella didn't think she could ever truly despise her mother. She just wished Ronda had that same mentality. Ronda seemed to spew hate. It exuded through her entire being. What seriously bothered Annabella was that this rage and abhorrence would usually surface when money was at the forefront. Annabella would have gladly given up hope of having anything material if she could've simply had her family again. Annabella just wanted things to go back to the way they used to be. Unfortunately, her hopes of that happening were fading considerably with each passing day.

10

FIGHT OR FLIGHT

Ronda and Annabella's relationship was worse than it had ever been. Ronda still didn't seem to particularly like Annabella. Annabella wished her mom would learn to trust her and treat her like Shanna's parents treated her. They gave her freedom and seemed to have confidence that the values that they had instilled in their daughter would ensure that she would not disappoint them. Annabella had never been in any real trouble, she got good grades and for the most part, she did what Ronda told her to do. This should have been good enough but Ronda would often find reasons to pick on Annabella. Ronda was not a nurturing and informed mother and she seemed to believe that the only way she could keep Annabella in line was through violence.

Early one afternoon, Annabella was sitting on the living room couch of their apartment having a snack. She was flipping through channels when there was a knock at the door. It was three of her male friends from school. They were on their bikes. Annabella had known these boys since the fifth grade and she had never shown romantic interest of any kind in any of them. They were like her annoying brothers.

"Hey Belly!" "You got some water or juice or something?" The boys were sweating profusely. It must have been 100 degrees in the Louisiana heat. Annabella knew she wasn't supposed to have boys inside the house but she felt badly for them. Plus, they'd only stay for ten minutes. Ronda wouldn't be home for about another hour and a half. "Come on in y'all." Annabella went to the kitchen and grabbed three juice boxes from the refrigerator. "So y'all just riding bikes?" Annabella asked, handing them the drinks as they stood next to their bikes. "Yeah, we're gonna ride to Chad's so we can whip his butt at some "Killer Instinct" one of the boys said with a chuckle. Annabella laughed too as she sat down on the couch and began flipping through the TV channels again. She got to MTV and stopped. The number one music video was playing. She turned up the volume and the kids all began singing along. During her enjoyment, Annabella didn't hear Ronda pull up with her squeaky brakes as she usually did, nor did she hear Ronda's key turn. As Ronda opened the door, the look of anger on her face looked horrific. Annabella knew she was going to get it. She immediately told the boys to leave. They did so posthaste with their bikes seeming to fly along with them. Dinah looked extremely scared for her little sister. Dinah had been working with Ronda at her cleaning service. Ronda had created the business while she and William were still married. She never saw much profit and considering the fact that she didn't need the money, she decided to close things down. She restarted it once she'd exhausted all her other possibilities of making money at the time. Dinah didn't do much but play games on the office computer and talk to her friends on the phone. This didn't seem to bother Ronda who paid her daughter as much as she would have offered a typical worker.

"So you're just a regular ol slut, ain'tcha?!?" Ronda screamed. "Mom, we weren't doing anything but watching....Ronda didn't give Annabella a chance to finish her sentence. She lunged at Annabella and began pulling her hair and punching and scratching her face. She pushed Annabella onto the couch and began to choke her. Dinah yelled for their mom to stop and she complied only to return from the kitchen with a wooden broom that she began beating Annabella with the stick end of. Annabella would cover one area only to get hit either in another one or on her knuckles. Dinah screamed loudly and grabbed her mother's offending arm. Annabella thought that Ronda might redirect her anger toward Dinah but Dinah always seemed to be off-limits when it came to Ronda's ferocity. Ronda dropped the broom, went into her bedroom and slammed the door. Dinah ran to the kitchen to get her sister some ice. Annabella was crying hysterically and could barely catch her breath. "Shhh, it's okay. Don't cry sis. It's okay" Dinah kept saying calmly. Annabella didn't know why her mother had reacted so violently but she couldn't say she wasn't used to it.

About a week later, the scratches on Annabella's skin had turned to scabs and her bruises were now blue and purple. Ronda had barely uttered a word to her daughter. Annabella didn't care. She knew that there was no chance for them to ever have a mother-daughter bond. Annabella went over to her Dad's business to pay him a visit. He was going over an invoice with a client when she walked in so Annabella sat down on her favorite bench and waited for him to finish. "Hey Belly!" William said. "Hey Daddy." "What's the matter? You seem kinda sad" William asked. "I'm okay" Annabella replied, twiddling her thumbs. William looked down at Annabella's hands only to see that some of her knuckles were bruised. "What happened to your hands?" "Oh, it's nothing Daddy." William knew when Annabella was lying because she could barely look him in the eyes. William raised up the sleeves on Annabella's shirt only to see more injuries on his daughter. "Ronda did this; didn't she?" William asked sternly. Annabella remained silent. William stood up, sighed loudly and walked toward his desk. "Daddy. It's OK" Annabella said attempting to sound reassuring. "No baby. It's not, but don't worry about it. I'll take care of it."

Annabella loved hanging out and sleeping over at Dinah's apartment. Then again, she liked being anywhere but home most of the time. Annabella thought that Ronda was simply going to drop her off for a routine visit with her sister but Ronda had to talk to Dinah about something. Annabella was sure she wouldn't be interested in their conversation so she went to Cassidy's room to play with her. Annabella adored Cassidy. She was super cute and she hung onto Annabella's every word which was a huge compliment to a thirteen-year-old. Just as they finished preparing another awfully cooked dish on Cassidy's "Easy Bake Oven", there was a knock at the front door. "I'll get it!" Annabella yelled. Annabella opened the door to find a man and a woman dressed in business attire standing there. "Hello. Are you Annabella?" the woman asked. Ronda immediately came up behind her and demanded, "Who's asking?" "Yes ma'am. I'm Mackenzie Dobson and this is my partner Alfred Wiggins." We're with Child Protective Services." "We received some information and we have reason to suspect that there has been some abuse occurring in the home." Ronda seemed angry but also a bit confused. "Who exactly do you "suspect" is being abused?" Ronda asked, using air quotes. "Ma'am, we need to ask you and Annabella a few questions in order to complete our investigation." Ronda flung the door open so hard that it nearly hit the back of the wall. They walked to the dining room table and sat down. "Oh, make yourself at home!" said Ronda, condescendingly. Dinah, seeing the look on her mother's face, tried to intervene. "Look, this is *my* house, so anything that may or may not have went on, didn't happen here!" Dinah exclaimed. "We are aware of that ma'am but this address was listed on the complaint as well as the home address of Ronda and Annabella Garland." "We just want to make sure the child is safe in the household." "Child?" "Do you see how tall this girl is?" "Ma'am, the height of a child doesn't make her any less of a child" Ms. Dobson responded. Ronda rolled her eyes. Annabella was nervous. Thankfully, her injuries from the last encounter she had with Ronda weren't easily visible to the officers. They began to question Ronda only to get smug looks and rude responses in return. They figured that they wouldn't get anywhere with her so they directed their interrogation toward Annabella. "Annabella, has your mother ever hit you forcefully?" "Look!" shouted Annabella. "I'm fine!" "I don't want to go anywhere. I love my family!" This was true, only at that exact moment; Annabella realized that the family she was referring to didn't include her very own mother. The investigators eventually left. They didn't make it clear whether they believed Annabella or Ronda. Annabella feared they'd be back. She didn't want to be taken to foster care. She only wanted her mother to learn to love her someday.

One morning, Craig dropped Annabella off at William's office. Annabella knew that it was her father who had called CPS and while she wasn't angry with him and she knew that he was only trying to protect her, she wished that he had thought about the possible consequences. She decided not to question him about it. She only wanted to enjoy her time with her dad and not relive the incident. William had some clients to tend to before he and Annabella went to brunch. Annabella watched TV while waiting on her father to finish up. She loved her dad's office. He had great taste in furniture and his desk chair was so comfy. He also had a lot of interesting gadgets on his desk and shelves that Annabella loved to mess with. Annabella's favorite thing in William's office was a stuffed, Velcro doll. The male doll was dressed in a business suit with the word 'BOSS' written across its chest. Its arms, legs and head were detachable and Annabella loved rearranging the parts. She had played with that doll since she was a small child and doing so now still brought a smile to her face.

"Get out of here Ronda!" William yelled. Annabella jumped up from her Dad's chair and peeked out of the office window. She could see her mother attempting to push William out of her way. "Annabella, you'd better get your ass out here now!" she screamed. "Ronda, what the hell is wrong with you?" William shouted. "I didn't tell that girl she could come over here!" Ronda screamed. "She's my child too and she has every right to be here!" William yelled back. "I don't give a damn that she's your child!" "Besides, we're gonna be late for her doctor's appointment!" Annabella was confused. She never went to the doctor unless she was very ill. "Ok Ronda. Go ahead and take her but don't come over here barging in again." "I'm getting sick of this shit!" "Come on out baby girl." Annabella walked out of the room slowly. Ronda grabbed Annabella by the arm to hurry her along. William put his hand on the back of Annabella's shoulder. "See ya later Belly." "Love you." "I love you too Daddy." Ronda let out a groan as she and Annabella walked to the car. "Mom, why am I going to the doctor?" "I'm not even sick" asked Annabella. "Well, I figured since you had boys in my house and you're grown enough to call CPS on me, you must be doing *other* grown-up things too." "What are you talking about?" "What grown-up things?" Annabella asked. "Oh, don't act all innocent now." "Mom, if you're talking about sex, that's not true. I'm only 13, I've never had sex, I'm a virgin!" "Yeah, right! I guess we'll see, won't we?" said Ronda with a grimace.

They arrived at the doctor's office. The wait wasn't very long. Annabella looked around at all the people coughing and then at the fish tank against the wall. She wished, if only for a day, she could be one of those fish. She wanted to be anyone or anything besides whom and what she was. Annabella walked into Doctor Beasley's office. He was an elderly, Caucasian man with hairy arms and ears. He had a deep speaking voice and extremely thin, white hair. Annabella was told to go into the bathroom and change into a paper gown. She heard her mother and the doctor chitchatting but she couldn't make out what they were saying. Annabella came out of the bathroom and sat on the table. She thought that the doctor was going to draw blood and maybe ask her a couple of questions to determine her virginity, but instead, he instructed her to lie down on her back and open her legs. Annabella had never been examined down there before, so she had a hard time keeping her legs from instinctively closing. The doctor inserted two fingers deep into Annabella's vagina and began to move up and down, and then back and forth. Annabella began to cry silently. She not only felt humiliated and violated, but when she looked over at her mother, Ronda was fooling and shuffling around with paperwork in her briefcase like she didn't have a care in the world. Annabella suffered a great deal of pain that day in more ways than one and yet, it turned out by the doctor's own findings, Ronda had been completely wrong all along. Annabella felt numb toward her mother. In fact, she no longer felt she had one.

The dances at the local gym were always the talk of the town amongst teens in the area. The music was always awesome and for Annabella, it meant getting away from Ronda for three hours, which was the icing on the cake. Annabella would usually go with Shanna and although she was a bit of a wallflower, Annabella loved hanging out with her best friend. Annabella also had other friends that she could dance with if she felt so inclined. Annabella had asked Ronda if she could go to the upcoming dance two weeks before it was due to occur and although she was met with a harsh, "I guess so Annabella", a yes was a yes to Annabella's eager ears. Ronda had given Annabella the conditions of keeping her room and the kitchen clean, not getting into any trouble in school and making sure not to bring any bad grades home. Annabella thoroughly adhered to the chores and terms as her excitement increased. She picked out the perfect outfit-an athletic black and white Nike windbreaker jumpsuit with matching sneakers.

It had been over five years since the divorce and Ronda was still just as vindictive and angry as if it had occurred only yesterday. It was the evening before the dance and Annabella was on the phone with Shanna when Ronda arrived home. "Get off the phone Annabella." "Ok Mom. Shanna has me on hold. I'll get off when she comes back." "We're just talking about what we're gonna wear to the dance tomorrow." Shanna came back on the line. "Hey girl! I gotta go." "I'll see you at school tomorrow!" "Ok, bye!" Annabella began to sing and do a little 'cha-cha' around the living room. "I'm sooo excited... and I just can't hide it. I'm go-ing to the dance...and I think I like it!" Ronda never liked seeing anyone happy when she was having a bad day. All of the attention needed to be on her. If not, she'd find a way to make it so one way or another. "You ain't going to that damn dance" Ronda said mockingly. "Huh?" "What do you mean?" "You already said I could go. I did everything you told me to-plus more! I even did everyone's laundry!" Annabella's eyes began to well up with tears. "Have you lost your God damned mind? Who the Hell are you getting loud with?" Ronda shouted, getting up from her chair. "This isn't fair!" "You always want me to be sad and have no fun or life, just like you!" Annabella cried. Ronda eyes seemed to glow with redness. She grabbed Annabella by the collar and attempted to shove her to the floor. Annabella held her strength and refused to go down. Ronda punched the side of Annabella's face with all her might. Usually, Annabella would have run away crying...but not this time. This time, Annabella struck her mother back. Ronda's expression went from shock... to fury. What began as a downstairs tussle made its way to being an upstairs brawl without either of them ever realizing how. Joshua heard all the ruckus and came rushing out of the bathroom in a towel. Thankfully, he was able to stop Ronda who had nearly choked her daughter to death. Unsurprisingly, Annabella never made it to the dance on Friday and despite the new wounds she had acquired, Annabella was very proud of herself for finally standing up to her mother's abuse.

Craig and Dinah's relationship was clearly on the rocks. Craig was confused but he sensed that he and Dinah were increasingly growing apart. Dinah no longer seemed to want to spend any quality time with him. Suddenly, she preferred the company of others- mostly of the female persuasion. One friend in particular was Muffy. She and Dinah had been spending a great deal of alone time together although

Muffy herself was also married. Annabella saw the two of them behaving strangely by cuddling with one another and stroking each other's hair. Annabella finally got the nerve to ask her sister what was going on after she found a romantic letter that Dinah had written to Muffy. Dinah didn't deny that she and Muffy had shared intimate encounters. Dinah confessed to her sister that she was indeed a lesbian. Annabella asked her sister what that meant for her and Craig only for Dinah to reply, "Don't know, don't care."

Annabella had no problems with her sister being a lesbian. However, for some reason, Annabella was not very fond of Muffy. She, Annabella, Dinah and Craig had gone to a house party that included Craig's family and some mutual friends. Fourteen-year-old Annabella had gotten drunk and began to stumble around a bit. The night was winding down so the four of them decided to leave and go back to Dinah and Craig's place. Craig's friend Lester asked for a ride to his apartment on the way back. Craig drove with Dinah in the passenger seat. Muffy sat to the left of Annabella while twenty-six-year-old Lester sat on the right. Craig was blasting the music with the windows down. Annabella laid her head back and began to drift off. She then felt a hand creep over the top of her pants and inside her panties. Annabella froze immediately. She had known Lester since she was nine years old. "Why was he doing this?" Annabella felt confused and scared. Muffy looked over and covered Annabella's lap with her large jean jacket to assist in concealing Lester's pedophilic wrongdoing. Annabella wanted to yell to her brother-in-law and sister but Muffy made it all seem so normal. "They won't care anyway." "No one cares" Annabella thought. Lester exited the vehicle but not before licking his fingers and smiling. When they arrived back at Dinah and Craig's, despite Muffy knowing everything that had happened, they all went inside to bed. Annabella was the only one who didn't sleep.

Dinah began to invite many other women to her and Craig's apartment. Craig felt disrespected and humiliated. He didn't want to give up on his marriage but he was extremely unhappy. "I don't know what to do Belly" Craig admitted. "I love her very much but this is ridiculous." "It's like she's not even my wife anymore. "She's changed lil sis" Craig uttered, hanging his head. "I notice it too. Her eyes don't even look the same anymore" Annabella said with a sigh. "I know you've loved her since you guys were kids but you're a fool if you stay here." Craig was taken aback but he knew his sister-in-law was right. He trusted her advice. After all, Annabella and Dinah were once as close as two sisters could be. Craig appreciated Annabella's opinion and observations and after absolutely no protesting from Dinah, he moved out. Dinah attempted to blame the dissolution of their marriage on Craig and insisted that *he* had been the one who was unfaithful. Some people believed her contrived tales, but Annabella knew the truth. Ronda also knew what really happened. Yet and still, she was right there with her daughter spreading falsehoods and asking for monetary gain during the divorce proceedings. Like mother, like daughter. They were two peas in a delusional, manipulative pod.

Ronda and Dinah had left for work. It was summertime so Annabella and Cassidy were still asleep. Since the fight, Annabella had been staying at her sister's place quite often. Dinah had developed the habit of sneaking out of the window when she wanted Annabella and/or Ronda to watch Cassidy so she could spend time with her newfound friends. Dinah was now dating a girl who was referred to as "Sam". Annabella didn't think much of their relationship considering Dinah seemingly fell "in love" every other month like clockwork. One night, on a "Tequila Tuesday" that Dinah and fourteen- year-old Annabella had made a tradition, Dinah invited Sam over to join them. Annabella didn't like sharing her sister with all these new people. They once had a very close relationship and never needed anyone to enhance nor participate in it. This time, Sam arrived with a friend. Marvin, who was thirty-five, seemed like a very nice man. He brought some marijuana and an extra bottle of tequila. They all went to Dinah's bedroom that she once shared with her husband Craig, to watch a movie. During the film, they had partaken in several shots and two marijuana joints. Dinah and Annabella were in the middle of the king-sized bed with Sam and Marvin on the end of each of them. At one point, during the movie, Marvin broke into a freestyle rap and began to caress Annabella's thigh with his eyes closed. Being high and intoxicated, Annabella was taken aback, yet slow in her actual acknowledgment of the occurrence. When she realized what was happening, she tapped her sister's shoulder. Dinah was leaning to the side, kissing her girlfriend, so she was reluctant to turn over and concede to her sister's attempt at gaining her attention. When Dinah noticed what was going on, Annabella expected her to flip her lid and cause the night's festivities to come to an immediate end. Instead, she chuckled and went back to Sam for more lip-locking. Annabella shoved Marvin's hand from her thigh and left the room. Dinah never followed her nor asked if Annabella was okay. Dinah gave Annabella Marvin's phone number and told her to call him if she ever wanted some more free weed.

Sneaking out of the bedroom window to avoid her responsibilities became quite commonplace for Dinah. She had done it so often that she'd often forget to close let alone lock it. One morning, Cassidy was asleep in Dinah's bed while Annabella slept in the other room. Something urged Annabella to tell her young niece to come into the room with her to sleep until they were ready to get up for breakfast. Annabella and Cassidy were best buddies. Annabella saw the path that her sister was going down. She was allowing the women that she was dating to disrespect and degrade her. Annabella wanted Cassidy to know that she was worth so much more than that and that she deserved to be treated like the beautiful young lady Annabella knew Cassidy would grow up to be. Annabella was no stranger to being treated poorly but she made sure that she never let Cassidy see her fawn over or beg for the attention or affection of a boy. Cassidy went nearly everywhere with Annabella. When they'd go to the mall and a boy would come up to Annabella in a way that she deemed unfit, Annabella made sure to let Cassidy know to never give disrespectful, disgusting boys the time of day. Cassidy truly admired and respected Annabella and despite her own young age, Annabella tried her best to be there for her niece.

While Annabella and Cassidy slept, Annabella heard a noise coming from the other room. At first, she ignored it, but it only grew louder. Annabella gently shook Cassidy awake. Annabella whispered, "Cassie, I hear something. I'm gonna go see what it is." Lock the door behind me and no matter what, do NOT come out of this room." "Okay Teedie." *Teedie* was a term that people from Louisiana used for Aunt or Auntie. Before leaving the room, Annabella grabbed the Louisville Slugger bat that Ronda always kept by the bedroom door. Annabella slowly opened the door ensuring that Cassidy was right behind it, heeding her previous instructions. Annabella turned the corner only to find two young, African American males attempting to rip Dinah's cable box and VHS player from the entertainment center.

"Get the Hell out of my house!" Annabella yelled, holding up the bat in a swinging position. Annabella had no idea where the instantaneous, bravery had come from, but apparently, it was successful. The robbers dropped what they were doing the second they saw her, running and toppling over one another. Annabella wondered how they had gotten in. Suddenly, she remembered Dinah's late-night escapades through the window. Annabella immediately ran to Dinah's bedroom to close and lock it. She then frantically picked up the phone and called Ronda and Dinah at the office. "Mom! Some guys just broke into the house!" "Are y'all okay?" Ronda asked. "Yes but hurry up. OK? We're scared!" "We'll be there in like 20 minutes" Ronda replied. "Should I call Dad until y'all get here?" "Why do you always wanna call your damn Daddy every time something happens?" Annabella didn't respond. William always made her feel safe. Annabella believed that a girl should always call her father if ever she felt afraid, especially of a man. Ronda hated for William to be involved in anything, unless of course, she were the one to call him. "Don't call *that man*. We'll see y'all in a minute." "Go ahead and call the police until we get there." Annabella did not like involving police unless absolutely necessary. However, she did as she was told. Dinah and Ronda got to Dinah's apartment before the police did. Dinah seemed nervous and a bit on edge. The Detectives arrived- an older Black male and a younger, Hispanic male. The Black male, Detective Steele and the Hispanic male, Detective Baez, arrived approximately thirty minutes later. Detective Steele walked in just ahead of Detective Baez and immediately began to look around. Baez was more anxious, as if it were his first day on the job. "So where are the suspects?" asked Steele. "There aren't any suspects here anymore" Annabella exclaimed. "I wasn't talking to you, young lady" Steele responded. "My niece and I were here when they broke in" said Annabella. "They came in through the window and tried to take stuff from the entertainment center." Detective Baez walked into Dinah's bedroom to check the window. A minute later, he walked out and announced that the window was not opened. "I closed and locked it after they ran out" Annabella explained. "I see" Steele replied. "It seems to me that this may have been an inside job. It was probably some of her little friends" Steele told Baez. "What? Why would I do something like that? Why would I call you guys if that were the case? I would never steal from my sister!" Annabella yelled. Annabella waited for Dinah to say something but she seemed to be afraid to admit that if it weren't for her recently sly and forgetful ways, the window wouldn't have been left open in the first place, putting her daughter and sister in danger. Baez seemed confused. "Nah-Nah"..."Tell these idiots how dumb they sound right now!" Annabella yelled. "Shut up Annabella! Go to the room!" Ronda screamed. "Fuck that!" "Why would he say something like that?" "Young lady, you'd better pipe down!" Steele yelled. "I'm calling my Daddy and he'll get this straight right away!" "You ain't calling no-damn-body!" "Go to the room now!" Ronda yelled. "Y'all are the dumbest cops I've ever seen!" "This is stupid!" Annabella ran to the bedroom with Cassidy right behind her. Cassidy was an awesome kid and hugged her Aunt snugly. They both knew what had happened. Unfortunately, the culprits were never apprehended and Annabella's mother nor sister, stuck up for her despite knowing the absolute truth. Annabella's feelings never seemed to matter much.

11

THE LAST MAGNOLIA

Annabella was finally allowed to go on dates. These weren't the typical dates where she was allowed to be picked up in a car by a particular boy but rather, they were group dates which seemed to be the more acceptable outings beginning to be tolerated by most of the parents of Annabella's friends. One night Shanna, her cousin Kaylee, Annabella and one other girl decided to go to the mall with four boys. The pack did their usual perusing of CD and shoe stores. They were having a decent, yet expectedly awkward teenage time. At the Redwood Mall, there was a drugstore that the kids would frequent often before using the nearby pay phones to call and be picked up. Annabella and Shanna loved gummy bears and went inside to see if there were any new flavors on the shelves. William walked in through a second, nearby entrance with his son-in-law, Herbert. Herbert was William's oldest daughter, Anastasia's husband. William, as usual, was buying alcohol and he seemed to be already intoxicated. William had previously gotten into a bad argument with Annabella and she vowed to never speak to him again. As she and Shanna walked by with their refreshments, William grabbed Annabella's arm tightly. "Hey baby!" Annabella jerked her arm away and proceeded to throw the now unwanted candy onto an adjacent rack. Shanna followed suit and they began to walk out of the store. Herbert muttered something to William and he became infuriated. While the kids were calling for their rides, they saw William come walking angrily and quickly out of the store. He grabbed Annabella by both of her arms, lifting her off of the ground. He slammed her skinny body between the payphones and against the wall repeatedly. Annabella was not contemplating her next move but something inside boiled her blood. She began kicking and screaming. Before she knew it, she had kicked William in his nether region. He immediately dropped her and looked at her in disbelief. He walked away shocked with Herbert behind him. Shanna and the rest of Annabella's friends ran to her aid in fear and unsure of what to do.

Annabella never grasped why her father chose to hang out with Herbert in the first place. He was an idiot in Annabella's eyes. After having only met William a handful of times, Herbert thought it would be a good idea to try and wrestle a loaded gun from him after several warnings to refrain from doing so. He ended up with a missing thumb and a bruised ego that never seemed to get any better. He was also a pervert. Only months prior, William had taken Annabella to visit some old friends and family that she hadn't seen in a while. Annabella had grown a few inches, and she was coming into her own as a fourteen-year-old young lady. William was proud of his beautiful, intelligent daughter and he really enjoyed seeing her bond with their loved ones. On their last stop, William decided to go to William Jr.'s and Klaudette's house. Technically, it wasn't their house but a close relative's. William Jr. had begun to spiral downward and spent most of his time drinking, smoking and fighting dogs. Klaudette had grown tired of his antics. "Still not gettin' none, ay son?" William Sr. chuckled. "Nope!" "But I still got my right hand." The duo laughed. "Hey man, forget that. Look what the cat drug in!" said William. "Hey sis!" "Hey big bro!" Annabella shouted, awaiting a bear hug. Herbert was sitting on the couch and Annabella could feel his eyes all over her. She ignored him and hoped that it was all her imagination. "I'm gonna go up and see Klaudette and the kiddos." Klaudette's greeting was welcoming but not joyful. Klaudette was not the usual happy-go-lucky young woman she once so effortlessly was and Annabella could tell that Klaudette was nearly at her breaking point with William Jr. "How are things going sis?" asked Annabella. "Fine, I guess. I'm just tired of your damn brother." What's going on? Are you two OK?" "Girl, no we're not. All he ever does is play with and fight those damn dogs." "He's even had a few killed. I don't want this for my family. Something has to change or I don't know what I'm gonna do." "Well, hopefully it's just a stupid phase and you guys can work things out" said Annabella. "Maybe" exclaimed Klaudette, hanging her head.

Annabella went back downstairs. After her sad and somewhat awkward exchange with Klaudette, she was ready to leave. She was supposed to be having fun and seeing her family fall further apart was definitely not her idea of a good time. William Jr. wanted to go out for drinks after their dad dropped Annabella off back at Ronda's. Herbert was standing against the wall adjacent to the front door. William Sr. and Jr. were already outside about to get into the car. As Annabella walked toward the door to make her exit, Herbert tried to touch her arm. She dodged his hand just as he whispered, "you shole is a fine ass lil thang." Annabella dashed outside. She so desperately wanted to tell her father and brother but she couldn't. She chalked it up to him being drunk and stupid. She knew William would kill him and as long as he never became violent or sexually forceful, Annabella would keep quiet. Thankfully, there was never another encounter.

The day after the mall incident, Annabella called William's office phone and left a very scathing message on his answering machine. She was hurt in many ways and she wasn't afraid or about to let William forget it. William let anyone he felt was important listen to it and they all thought that Annabella was the most disrespectful child in existence. William had a way of only telling part of a story and usually it was the part that made him look like less than the giant jerk he could be at times. Time went on and as usual, Annabella missed her father and yearned to reconnect with him. She could never stay mad at him. Annabella realized that her father had been through a lot and she could sense the sadness within him. She could also clearly see it in his eyes. No matter how happy he seemed to be, she could always look into his dark brown, nearly black colored eyes and see the tears that were just dying to be allowed to escape without judgment. Vietnam had certainly done a number on him both physically and mentally and his brutal childhood seemed to only set fire to the embers currently on the surface. Annabella could almost feel William's pain as if it were her own making it difficult for her to cut him off altogether even when he was clearly in the wrong regarding most, if not all their current issues. Still, Annabella was growing tired of giving her father passes. She needed him to be there for her especially because of the way things were with her and Ronda. At that time in her life, if she didn't have William, she didn't have anyone.

A few months later, Annabella decided to pay her father

a surprise visit at his office. She had gotten heavily into writing and poetry was at the forefront of her expression. She rang the bell. William seemed pleased to see her. Instead of inviting her to come inside, William stepped out and walked Annabella over to his tree and flower garden. There, once again, were those big magnolia flowers that were magnified in fragrance by the moisture in the air. William placed one in Annabella's hair as he had usually done when she'd come to visit. "How are you Daddy?" asked Annabella. "I'm fine baby. Come inside." Annabella followed her father but she could sense that he wasn't exactly in the right frame of mind. "Daddy, I've been writing poetry and I want you to read my last poem. "Sure" replied William with a stoic glare. The two of them walked inside. As William began to read the poem which happened to be about his and Annabella's recently very rocky relationship and the way she believed William had become, William's expression changed both drastically and immediately. William finished the poem and tossed the paper on top of the front desk. "It's a nice poem but it's not true." "What do you mean it's not true Daddy?" asked Annabella. "Come into the office" William said sternly. William plopped down into his heavy, yet posh office chair and looked piercingly at Annabella. "Look, I don't like the way your attitude has been lately." "You have no respect for me anymore." Annabella could tell that her father was upset but she thought that they would at least be able to work through their issues and move on. "I don't know what you want me to say but I don't think I've done anything wrong" Annabella replied, staring right into her father's eyes. "I will whoop your butt!" William yelled. "Daddy I love you but I'm not afraid of you." This angered William a great deal. He seemed to thrive off people being afraid of him. He was a very big and intimidating man, yet Annabella still saw him as her loving father. While she respected him to the best of her abilities, she did not fear him in the slightest. "Well, since you're so tough, get out of my damn building and don't you ever come back!" William stood up as Annabella looked at him in disbelief. It was now pouring raining outside and the wind was howling fiercely. "Let me call my Mom to come get me." "No! I don't want that damn woman over here. Get your ass out now!" Annabella had her pride that she had ironically always believed came from her father. She seemed to have grown cold to being treated so harshly. Annabella grabbed her bag and raced out the door. The rainstorm had gotten treacherous but Annabella just wanted to get as far away from her dad as she possibly could. As she got far enough away, she began to sob uncontrollably. She was terrible with directions and had no idea how to get back to Dinah's apartment. She, Ronda and Josh had been staying there ever since Ronda failed to pay rent multiple times and they were evicted from their place. As the eye liner-mixed tears rolled down Annabella's cheeks, she could barely see in front of her. There was a truck following behind Annabella that refused to pass her in the street. A bald, pudgy African American man pulled the vehicle over and asked Annabella if she wanted a ride. Although Annabella knew the dangers of getting inside a stranger's vehicle, she decided to take him up on his offer. She figured that if no one, especially her own father cared about her, why should she care about herself? She hopped into the lovely upholstered truck. "Hey. My name's Raymond." "What's yours?" "Annabella" she replied. "Nice to meet you Annabella." "That's a nice flower you've got there." "A magnolia? Right?" "Yeah" Annabella replied softly. "Where ya headed?" he asked with a creepy grin. "I need to get to my sister's house" said Annabella. Annabella gave him the address and his expression indicated that he knew exactly where that was. They drove for about ten minutes before Raymond pulled over. "Why are we stopping?" Annabella asked nervously. "Well, I just wanted to let you know that if you need anyone or anything that I can be here for you." He began to stroke Annabella's leg. "You are such a beautiful little girl and you only deserve happiness." Annabella was terrified and she knew that this man did not have her best interest at heart. Annabella quickly pushed his hand away and shot him a scathing glance. Raymond became quite angry and suddenly, his hand was wrapped tightly around a chunk of Annabella's hair as he forcefully pulled her head back. Annabella began to replay what had just happened with her and William in her head. Something deep within wanted her to allow Raymond to do what he wanted with her and leave her in a ditch. She didn't want to live anymore and perhaps dying this way would show her parents and everyone else the horrible mistakes they'd made that led up to this very moment. She closed her eyes and finally, she felt free. "Go ahead!" "I don't give a fuck!" For some reason, this confused and startled Raymond, causing him to release his grasp. Without thinking, Annabella jumped out of the truck. She ran as fast as she could to Dinah's, throwing the last magnolia her father would ever put in her hair onto the soaking wet concrete. She got home and wrote the deepest, saddest poem she could find within her. She was truly broken inside.

Annabella didn't feel very well the next day. She was so tired and depressed that she could barely roll out of the bed to use the bathroom. She felt so miserable. Her insides seemed hollow. She told Dinah what had happened and they talked about William's actions over the years. However, Annabella didn't believe that anything would make her feel better. Two days later, Annabella went out to Ronda's car to find a lovely, colorful bouquet of flowers. There was a card that read: "To my loving daughter from Daddy." Annabella wasn't surprised that William hadn't specifically apologized. It was never in his nature to do so. Annabella gathered the card and bouquet and threw them into the apartment dumpster. Even if he *had* apologized, Annabella wasn't sure that she would've accepted it. She needed time to think and she wondered if she'd ever have the father she once knew and adored back in her life again.

12

NO MENDED ENDINGS

Joshua, now twenty years old, had been sporadically living on his own for a couple of years. He would only come back around when he failed to maintain his own place, got arrested or just wanted food and a place to crash. He also totaled two of his own used cars due to driving drunk and high. He would finagle his way back in merely to talk Ronda out of her car keys. Ronda was hesitant about him using her only mode of transportation other than her beat up work van but she also made him pick up and drop off Annabella at certain places when she didn't feel like being bothered to do so.

Annabella, Shanna and Kaylee decided to go to the movies. Joshua also drove them to pick up Annabella's on again, off again childhood boyfriend Juarez, on the way there. Annabella cared a great deal for Juarez, but she knew she could never be with him long term. He had too many unresolved issues and insecurities to ever love Annabella the way she needed to be loved. Juarez often demeaned and even got physical with her a few times. Annabella was only fourteen years old but deep down, she knew the type of man she'd marry and build a life with. She didn't see Juarez ever growing into being that man and she knew she never would. For now, she was just young and having fun. She was enjoying simply being a teenager. Once they arrived at the movies, the kids went and got their snacks at the concession stand. They saw some other friends at the theatre and decided to expand their little group. The movie ended, and after playing some arcade games, they cruised the attached mall and talked about teenaged nothingness per usual.

After saying their goodbyes to the other teens, the foursome waited outside for Joshua to pick them up. After about thirty minutes, Annabella called Ronda from a payphone. "Mom, Josh isn't here yet." Well what do you want me to do about it Annabella?" "I was just wondering if he called you to let you know if he was on his way or not." "Nope. He hasn't" "I thought you liked hanging out with your little funky friends anyway and staying out all night." "Shouldn't you be jumping for joy?" Ronda chuckled. "It's not that Mom. Shanna and Kaylee have a curfew and need to get home soon." "At least they respect *their* parents." "Okay Mom. I guess I'll just wait." "Well, you don't have much of a choice; now do you?" Annabella always felt that her mother wanted to argue with her and with both of their tempers having the possibility to erupt at any moment, Annabella always tried her best to avoid confrontation if possible.

Another fifteen minutes went by and finally, Annabella saw Joshua pulling up in Ronda's car. The stereo system was cranked way up and marijuana smoke flowed from the windows. Reluctantly, Annabella and her three friends approached the vehicle. Once they got to the car, they realized that Joshua had company. There were two sketchy-looking young men with him. One was sitting in the passenger seat and the other was seated in the middle of the backseat. Embarrassed and irritated, Annabella asked, "Joshua, where the hell are we supposed to sit?" Obviously high, he replied, "Y'all can find a spot". A Honda Civic wasn't exactly what one would refer to as a roomy vehicle. Yet, Joshua was behaving as if it were a minivan. "Look, you sit on Juarez's lap and Kaylee or Shanna can sit on my homie's lap" Joshua slurred. "Have you lost your damn mind? Why don't you tell your gross friends to take a hike?" Annabella yelled. "Just get your ass in the fuckin' car!" "Come on Belly, we'll make it work" exclaimed Shanna worried about both curfew and Joshua and Annabella exploding on one another. Kaylee ended up sitting on Shanna's lap and Annabella sat on Juarez's. The random sleazeballs remained as they were. Annabella was fuming by the time they dropped Juarez off at his house. Shanna and Kaylee were being dropped off together. By the time they got remotely close to their destination, Annabella wanted to strangle Joshua. The music was obnoxious, their breath could gag a maggot and the weed smoke was certainly going to be hard to explain to the parents of Annabella's friends. Annabella and her peers were no angels but they at least believed in a certain degree of discretion and respect when it came to such things. Suddenly, one of Joshua's friends yelled, "Pull over in this complex, right here!" Annabella and her friends all looked at each other in disbelief. "Joshua what are you doing? They've gotta get home!" "Just chill in the car for a little while. I'll be right back" Joshua garbled. He followed his two unpleasant associates into the doorway of someone's apartment. It was now 10:45 pm and Annabella's friends had still not made it home. "I'm sorry about this you guys. I'll go see if I can get him to hurry up." Annabella got out of the car and walked toward the door that she saw Joshua go into. As she neared it, her brother reappeared. Relieved, she said, "Finally! Come on. Let's go." "Naw, I ain't ready to go yet. I'm handling something right now." Joshua always liked to pretend that he was tougher, more popular and more street savvy than he ever was or ever could be. It seemed to make him feel cooler and more masculine. "Are you kidding me? We have to go now!" Suddenly, Joshua threw the car keys toward Annabella. "Here! You fuckin' drive then!" The keys landed behind her in the darkness while Joshua trotted back toward his friends. "I can't believe him. He's such a fuckin' asshole!" "Help me look for the keys guys." "None of us know how to drive" Shanna replied. "I know that but we still have to find them" Annabella said exhaustedly. After about ten minutes of looking around all to no avail, Joshua came walking sluggishly toward the car. "Come on, let's go." "Where the keys at?" "You threw them into the dark." "Remember?" Annabella said angrily. "You didn't catch em?" Joshua asked drunkenly. "Um no, dumb ass!" Annabella replied with an eye roll. "You'z a dumb bitch!" Joshua yelled. "*I'm* a dumb bitch?" "You're the one who threw keys in a dark ass, ghetto parking lot! We can't drive anyway you damn moron!" Without warning, Joshua punched Annabella directly in her face. After checking her lip for blood, Annabella swung back landing a right hook to her brother's cheek. They began trading punches like they were not only strangers, but mere enemies. After breaking free from one another, Joshua continued to call Annabella derogatory names while crouching down looking for the keys he'd thrown. Annabella saw this as a chance to take him down. She ran forward with all her might and kicked Joshua square in the back of his testicles. To her surprise, it didn't hurt him in the slightest. It did, however, infuriate him much further. He abruptly stood up, grabbed Annabella by the shoulders, and rammed her into the corner of the open car door. Annabella hit the ground and began to cry in agony. Shanna and Kaylee had watched in disbelief through the entire ordeal. Yet, they saw their friend's fall as their chance to intervene. "It's ok. It's ok" said Shanna. "Let's just walk to our Aunt's house. It's like fifteen minutes away. My mom and dad are there". Annabella wished her pals had revealed that information earlier but the incident gave Annabella the chance to see how far Joshua had fallen and that he truly needed some help. Shanna's parents gave Annabella a ride home. Ronda didn't seem to care much at all about the incident. She made Annabella some eggs and told her to go take a hot bath. Ronda always figured that Annabella had instigated it in some way. Ronda took everyone's side over Annabella's. When Ronda was bored and not obsessing over William or some hair-brained scheme, she loved to try and monitor Annabella's every move. She loved telling Annabella "no" to ruin her day all while turning a blind eye to anything else that was going on.

Months after the parking lot incident, Ronda moved the three of them to a house in Marrero. This is when Joshua began a sexual relationship with a fourteen-year-old girl. He'd sneak her in late at night. She even slept over a few times. Ronda didn't seem to notice or maybe she just didn't care. But when Annabella wanted to simply talk on the phone with her friends, Ronda would listen in. She would search Annabella's room and throw away things she didn't like. She invaded Annabella's privacy every chance she got. Ronda never knew that Joshua's twenty-eight- year-old friend had kissed and threatened to rape Annabella. When Annabella told Joshua, he accused her of lying. Annabella figured her mother wouldn't care anyway. So, like most of the things that scared or saddened her, Annabella kept it locked tightly away from the one person she should have been able to turn to.

Dinah was finally beginning to feel like one of the in-crowd. She was getting invited to parties and was going to clubs with what she called her new "family." She seemed to think she was important when she was with them. Annabella often wondered if she would have been given so much attention and "love" if she weren't constantly shelling out money, paying for all their drinks and showering them with gifts, often at the expense of her own family. Ronda had five buildings that she cleaned regularly. One building in particular, was one that she not only cleaned, but it was also the one in which her own office was located. Annabella, Joshua and Dinah also helped her clean these buildings since there was no way Ronda was going to pay a crew when she had her able-bodied children to do the work. One night while cleaning, a check for $2,500 went missing. The next day, Ronda received a call from the owner of the building stating that she was being accused of stealing the check. Ronda immediately began to curse and scream at Joshua. He denied taking the money but due to his reputation, no one believed him. Ronda called him a drugged-out, good for nothing loser quite frequently. A few days later, Dinah admitted to Annabella that she had taken the check but that she was too scared to try to cash it. Over a week had gone by and Ronda continued to accuse Joshua. Annabella had a certain amount of devotion to Dinah but she and Joshua had also begun to grow closer. He had apologized for what he'd done and they were beginning to move past it. They actually had a lot of fun together. Annabella felt that it was completely unfair to blame Joshua. She decided to tell her mother, with the four of them in the room, what really happened. "Mom, Dinah was the one who took the check." Joshua and Annabella looked at each other, hoping for once, Dinah would finally get disciplined, chastised or downgraded for her actions. Instead, Ronda just looked at Dinah. Dinah didn't bother to apologize, nor did Ronda demand one. She simply sighed and walked out of the room.

Ronda rarely showed anger towards Dinah. She was the only child Ronda seemed to not only truly love but she actually liked her as well. Annabella could count on one hand the amount of times Ronda had raised her voice at Dinah. Ronda and Dinah had gotten in a car accident while driving home from work together. The driver in the other car was at fault but in order to get the highest amount of compensation possible, Ronda and Dinah would have to see doctors and chiropractors for several months to a year. Annabella accompanied them to one of their visits after they had picked her up from school. Ronda was still being seen in one room while Dinah was in another. Upon exiting, Annabella realized that Dinah was distraught with tears in her eyes. She stormed out of the office entrance. The door to the exam room was still open so Annabella could see inside. The female chiropractor and the male nurse had looks of disgust on their faces. The nurse then began to spray a profuse amount of air freshener in the air. Dinah's hygiene was never the best and unfortunately, it had gotten worse with all her weight gain. Ronda would hint at smelling something "fishy" or "shitty" while Dinah was around but she would never talk to Dinah directly about it. Annabella ran after Dinah to talk to her only to find her sobbing in the car. Annabella thought it'd be best if she gave her sister some space. Once Ronda was finished, she and Annabella got back into the car. Dinah was no longer crying. She just stared out of the window and watched the cars and seemingly the world go by. "What's wrong witchu my baby?" Ronda said while driving out of the parking lot. "Nothing Ma" Dinah said somberly. "Did you get your appointment slip?" "We've gotta come back on Thursday." "I'm not going back" Dinah replied sharply. "What are you talking about girl?" Ronda said, taking her eyes off the road and placing them on her daughter. "Mama, those people are assholes." "What happened?" "I don't wanna talk about it. I just don't want to go back!" "Girl, you're gonna make us miss out on all that money?" "For what?!?" Dinah remained quiet. "You shole is a dumb ass girl!" Ronda yelled. Dinah began to cry. "It's OK sis" Annabella said, rubbing her sister's shoulder from the backseat. "No it ain't OK." "You gonna miss out on some money for some dumb shit! I don't ev...." "They said I stink! OK?" "Are you happy now?" Ronda was shocked into silence. "So, just take a bath before you go from now on" Ronda said in a low tone. Ronda was fuming but she decided not to press the issue. Ronda loved lawsuits even if she had to subject herself or anyone else to inconvenience, lost time and even humiliation. For a little while, Ronda and Dinah's relationship was a bit awkward, especially at work, but things soon went back to normal for the two of them.

Dinah's attitude and behaviors became more distant and erratic. One night, Dinah, Annabella, Cassidy and a friend of Dinah's were going out. Dinah's neighbor, an Active-duty Airman, had just gotten out of his car. He said hello to the ladies, just as he had done on several other occasions as he walked up the steps to his apartment. Annabella saw Dinah reach down toward the ground. In her hand, was her neighbor's wallet. Annabella thought her sister would go upstairs right away and return his property. Yet, instead, a look of pure glee travelled across her face. Not only did she not return his identification cards, including his military ID, she took the cash that was in his wallet along with his credit cards and went on a shopping spree that night at the mall. She only stopped once the cards got declined. Luckily for her, they weren't reported stolen at that time. Dinah had offered to purchase some items for Annabella but Annabella declined. Annabella couldn't fathom how nonchalant Dinah was about the whole thing. Dinah continued to smile and converse with her neighbor until he moved out of the complex. He never seemed to suspect a thing. Dinah continued on a similar path for years to come.

Ronda and Annabella's relationship was more tumultuous than ever. They were arguing nearly every day and Annabella was unsure just how much more she could endure. No one believed how bad it had become and most were holding the assumption that Annabella was simply a wild, rebellious sixteen- year-old. Annabella yearned to love her mother but she just didn't know how. So many things had occurred leaving scars upon both her body as well as her fragile, juvenile psyche. All Annabella felt she could accomplish was to basically keep her distance and hope that eventually, everything would fall into place.

One night, after coming home from the mall, Annabella decided to take a hot shower before watching a little television and going to bed. Annabella loved taking showers. It was her way to feel as if her sorrows were being drowned out and washed away all at the same time. She would often let the tears that she felt would be ridiculed by others, fall away from her eyes and into the abyss where she wished to keep them hidden forever. Annabella sat down into the bathtub with the water beading upon her body. She only wished that she could make the water forceful enough to pierce through the exterior that everyone had faultily mistaken as toughness and strength. In truth, she was still that little girl whose childhood had been brought to a screeching halt and then ripped away. Annabella never wanted to dim anyone's light around her. Instead, she chose to embellish her own, with hopes that someone, somewhere would understand.

After drying off and putting on her t-shirt and cartoon themed boxers that were oh so popular among teenaged girls, Annabella poured herself into bed and despite her avid childhood insomnia, she managed to shut down her innermost thoughts and drift off to sleep. Suddenly, she was awakened by a light at her bedroom door. Ronda was standing there with an aura around her that confusingly seem to only darken the room. "Wake your ass up!" Ronda yelled. "Mom? What's the problem?" asked Annabella, her hand over her brow. "Oh, so you can neeeever sleep but as soon as ya mama wanna talk to ya, you're sooooo sleeeepy." "Mom, what are you talking about?" "I found that little poem you wrote about being so sad and unhappy." "What'd I ever do to yyoouu, huh?" Ronda stuttered. "Nothing Mom. I just want to go to bed." "No, you're not going no-damn-where!" Ronda slurred. Annabella figured her mother was either drunk or feeling the effects of the meds a doctor had prescribed Ronda for her depression. Annabella was wary of medicine that changed a person's brain or mood but at the time of the prescription, she was relieved that Ronda would have something that could possibly help her calm down and perhaps take away even some of the anger and disdain that Ronda seemed to constantly carry from the very sight of her daughter. "Mom, just get out of my room! Please!" Annabella pleaded. Her statement only put a match to Ronda's seething vitriol. Suddenly, Ronda ran swiftly to Annabella's bed and gripped her throat with one hand, revealing a knife in the other. "You love yo damn Daddy soooo much-huh? You must wannn-na be juuust like him?" "How a-bout I treeeat you like em?" Ronda began sloppily kissing Annabella's face. Annabella tried to fight her mother off but Ronda's eyes had never looked emptier, her soul, never more vacant. This was the second time her mother had pulled a knife on her and Annabella knew this was it. Ronda was finally going to take Annabella's life like she had repeatedly reminded Annabella how her birth had almost taken hers. Oddly, something within told Annabella that she had a reason to live, a purpose to go on. She managed to battle her inner urge to let it all go as she swung Ronda to the left side of her and onto the floor. "Mom! Stop it!" Annabella screamed. Momentarily, Ronda came back to reality with tears welling within her eyes. "You ain't shit you little bitch." Ronda got up and staggered out of Annabella's room. After waiting a few seconds and catching her breath, Annabella got up and closed and locked the door. Annabella curled herself into a ball on her bed, sobbing hysterically. She hoped that she could just cry herself to sleep and pretend that this nightmare hadn't actually indeed been a certainty. Unfortunately, that never happened. Still, Annabella never told a soul. Ronda was beginning to make daily threats about kicking Annabella out as soon as she turned eighteen. Annabella had been rebellious and intermittently unmotivated in her late teen years. She neither had the drive nor the support to keep going. She was exhausted.

Annabella finally decided to attend an out-of-state trade school. She did quite well. Nadine lived nearby and was a big help and support system. Annabella also met Ernesto, the love of her life there. He was a ray of sunshine during days that were beginning to only get darker as time went on and although he was too good to be true in Annabella's eyes, she let him love her anyway. It was the best decision that Annabella ever made in her young life. Annabella was confused why someone like him could or would ever love someone like her but little did Annabella know, Ernesto felt exactly the same way about himself. The two mistakenly undeserving lovers were inseparable from the moment they agreed to officially belong to one another.

Dinah was in a very dire situation. Everything that she had worked so hard to gather and maintain was crumbling right before her eyes. Her most recent girlfriend had just dumped her after discovering stacks of delinquent credit card notices accompanied by a severely lowered credit score. Dinah had also started to date men on the side to fund her social endeavors, which certainly was not tolerable in a strictly lesbian community. Craig had gotten remarried to a wonderful woman. They moved to Idaho with their two children where they bought a decent amount of land on which to build their lovely home upon. Cassidy, now a young adult, visited them during the holidays and whenever else she got a chance. She loved having a stepmom and her Dad at home again. Dinah would often call Craig and say she wanted to work things out but he was happy. He loved his beautiful wife. Besides, he knew Dinah was only calling out of desperation.

One night, Dinah had gathered up just enough money to hang out with some friends at a local restaurant and bar. She would've spent her last dime just to be in the presence of anyone in the LGBT community. She had disappointed or wronged everyone who truly loved her. None of them could understand her constant need for the acceptance of these individuals. It was like a drug habit that she could never seem to nor want to kick. She did everything she could to look her best that night. She had regained quite a bit of weight due to not following the regulations of her doctor after having weight loss surgery. She was still much thinner than before but she was very unhealthy. Spanx and girdles seemed to do the trick but she knew that others could notice the change. She would often get catty remarks from so-called friends that seemed to put dents in her already unstable self-esteem. Yet, she had this longing to feel accepted and welcomed among her peers no matter what it took. Dinah arrived twenty minutes early. She was so excited to be out and about again. It took about ten phone calls to gather herself and two other ladies together but Dinah knew that tonight would be just what she needed. Once her company arrived, the awkwardness followed suit. Daquita played with her weave, Simone, twiddled her fingers. "Sooooo, you guys wanna order?" Dinah asked nervously. "Well, I don't really have too much money so I'm just gonna get a glass of water and an appetizer" Simone replied, kicking Daquita under the table. "Me too girl!" yelled Daquita, with a slight giggle. "Come on guys, I'll pay. We haven't seen each other in so long, I think we can do better than that!" said Dinah, flashing a big smile. "You're right girrrrl!" Simone replied. The food seemed to be the only thing keeping their dinner alive considering no one really talked. Dinah's guest preferred to stare off into space or look at themselves in their compacts. While the waiter was describing the desserts to Dinah, the other two ladies excused themselves to the restroom, ducking off into the handicapped stall. "Girl, can we leave already?" Daquita groaned. "Come on Quita, that's not right" replied Simone. "I know but she's soooo annoying!" "I mean, how damn pathetic can you be?" "We have never been close with her. We've never been friends. The only reason we even allowed her in our circle was because of her relationship with Taylor. I'm just over her." "You mean like how her stomach is hanging over her belt?" "I wonder how many desserts she's eaten by now?" The girls giggled. Little did they know that Dinah had heard everything they'd said. She didn't bother waiting for them to make an excuse to walk out on her. She left the restaurant and having spent cab fare and some of her rent money on dinner, she had no choice but to walk all the way back to her one-bedroom, unfurnished apartment, alone. She dragged herself to the bathroom in an attempt to get ready for bed but her energy was basically non-existent. She flopped onto her air mattress fully clothed and with makeup still on her face. She was drained. She was in her late forties and had nothing to show for it. She began to think about all she'd done to the people she was supposed to love, and all that she'd done to herself. She thought of Annabella and she wished she could just call and have her little sister back. Their relationship fell completely apart when Ronda became ill and was in dire financial need. Annabella asked Dinah to help out and Dinah blatantly refused. As a result, Annabella went into debt helping their mother. Dinah later opened a bank account in Annabella's name and used it to store fraudulent welfare funds. Their relationship was irreparable. Dinah thought about her mother and how she had only used Ronda for money instead of just being a loving daughter. Maybe she could've helped to get Joshua into a rehab facility instead of worrying about people she barely knew. She wished she could have taken everything back but it seemed to be too late. She had nothing left to give and no one left to take from. Feeling hopeless and dazed, she opened her purse to a bottle of anti-depressants and a half-flask of cheap gin. With a long sigh, Dinah took the entire bottle of medication in addition to her own life that night. Four people attended her funeral. None of them knew her personally.

"Hello Annabella baby." "Hi Ms. Tabby. It's been awhile. How are you?" "I'm not so good my dear. It's about William." "Well, what did he do *this* time? He's always doing something messed up to *somebody*" Annabella replied. "Your Daddy's gone!" Tabitha wailed into the receiver. William had been drinking heavily and listening to oldies all night. He hated the way his life had turned out. The pride that he once wore like a finely tailored suit had withered away to nothing more than a gas station t-shirt. His business had nearly failed completely. Crystal found a way to deplete any remaining cash that he did have. His guilt for not being able to supply her and Alice with everything he thought he could, ate at him daily. All he could do was try to drink the pain away. He got into his old truck that he once adored so much. The lights on the outside no longer worked and it had become the boss in deciding whether to actually start or not. He rode with the windows down belting, "If you think you're lonely nooooow....wait untiiiiil tonight, girrrrrl!" He wondered why he didn't do better and how he let it all slip away. William didn't realize how fast he was going or that he was travelling down a one-way street in the wrong direction. His truck collided with another vehicle. William, along with two teenagers were killed instantly in the head-on collision. "Are you there?" Tabby asked. Annabella couldn't talk. She didn't know if she were even still breathing. She couldn't cry. She couldn't move. Along with her father, a part of Annabella's spirit died that day.

Annabella never knew why Joshua, who had so much potential to be a great Artist or Scientist, cared more about fitting in than simply being himself. Constant, frequently long jail and prison sentences had done severe damage to his mental health. During his sporadic incarceration releases, and sometimes after attaining them while still behind bars, drugs were the only things that quieted the voices and dulled or thwarted the pain. This never remedied his situation and instead, became a never-ending cycle of destruction. He had lost his only son in a custody battle. He also lost two other children due to his violence against their mother while they were still in utero. After moving to Grandburg and living with Ronda, he and Vivian had started smoking crack cocaine together. They even had an avid incestuous relationship that sent snickers and whispers floating around the small town. Everyone in the family swept it under the rug as they did most things. However, Annabella knew that she had lost her brother forever. She knew that he was too far gone to ever return. Joshua had exhausted all possibilities of being helped and was now a shell of his former young self. Not uncommon for him whatsoever, Joshua had broken into a supposedly unoccupied residence in hopes of finding something to pawn to fuel his habit. Joshua was never a hardened criminal, only a desperate, saddened one who typically posed no danger other than to himself. While going through the drawers of the occupant's bedroom, he was met with a 12-gauge shotgun to the chest. At the time, he and the family were estranged as usual. This included Annabella after he'd taken the last 20 dollars she had to her name from her purse. The anger she had toward him aside, she missed her big brother and always had a soft spot in her increasingly hardening heart for him. He was responsible for his own actions but Annabella knew that what had led to them, was not entirely his fault.

Ronda and Annabella never mended their broken relationship. After many one-sided attempts, Annabella conceded to defeat and realized that what never was, could simply and justifiably, never be. Ronda had spent all the money she'd gotten from the divorce settlements and her many other schemes. She had no other choice but to collect government aid and move in with her sister Shirley in their shabby little hometown. Even after the news had broken about William's accident, Ronda continued to roam the streets daily with plastic grocery bags full of paperwork showing passersby her "evidence" of injustices and William's wrongdoings coupled with her genius plot to once and for all reclaim what had been rightfully hers all along. Her obsessions were all she had left of the lifestyle she had worked so hard to make all those in her presence greenly envious of. Once in a while, she'd mention Annabella and say, "She's the only one who really loved me." "I miss that lil ol' girl." That message would sometimes be relayed to Annabella only to finally fall upon deaf ears. Annabella at one point felt sorry for her mother. But now, she merely felt nothing at all.

The last time Annabella had seen her father was at her and Ernesto's wedding. They were married in a small ceremony on the beach. Despite their consistent falling out, Annabella loved and respected William and still cared and valued his opinion a great deal. Not shockingly, during their first introduction, Ernesto and William formed an instant bond. William trusted his daughter's ability to choose a man that would love and protect her unconditionally. Ronda refused to attend the nuptials and festivities. Ronda despised Ernesto due to his unwillingness to force Annabella to continue to feed Ronda's rampant, delusional narcissism. No one could force Annabella to do anything and if Ronda would've tried to get to truly know her daughter, she would've known better than to believe otherwise. Ronda had insisted Ernesto was an undocumented immigrant despite him showing her his United States birth certificate. Ronda tried every trick in the book to tear them apart all to no avail. Ronda took her own failure at attempts to demolish the happiness of others as a personal challenge and attack. Ernesto was a very hardworking and honest man. He treated Annabella the way she finally found a way to allow herself to experience and deserve. Years after they wed, they won a large state lottery and retired early, moving out to the country with their four children. Annabella swore to never put her kids through even an inkling of the pain and dysfunction she endured as a child.

Annabella had never visited her father's grave before. She just couldn't bring herself to. Ernesto wanted to go with her that day but Annabella needed to confront everything she was feeling...the sadness, the anger, the trauma. Whatever she needed to do, she needed to do it alone. Annabella walked around a bit before she made her way toward her father's headstone. The air smelled of inevitable sorrow. She looked at all the people who'd been laid to rest as she pondered the unsettled pain and the many forgotten, unspoken apologies.

"Hi Daddy." Annabella said while placing a single magnolia atop her father's resting place. "I know how much you love these stinky ol' things" she chuckled tearfully. Annabella fell down to her knees and began to sob. "Daddy, what happened? Our family just fell apart!" Annabella began replaying in her mind what had happened to Ronda, Joshua and Dinah. She thought of how much she once took pride in her family and the days when she valued each and every moment they'd spent together. "Daddy, why couldn't you fix us?" "Why couldn't *I* fix us?" "Help me. Help me not to feel so lost!" Annabella knew she'd receive no answers. She simply had to find a way to keep going no matter how badly the grief was shattering her from the inside out. Annabella cried until she couldn't any longer. Somehow, she finally found the physical strength to stand back up. She'd never visit her father again. Upon rising, Annabella slowly looked up at the sky. There it was again. It had never looked so bright and beautiful-the clouds, so fluffily white. Yep. It was true, just as she'd suspected. The sun hated her alright. Only now and forever... she hated it right back.

Lightning Source UK Ltd.
Milton Keynes UK
UKHW012017080621
385174UK00001B/42

9 781977 242884